THE INVADERS

THE INVADERS

KAROLINA WACLAWIAK

Regan Arts.

NEW YORK

Regan Arts.

65 Bleecker Street
New York, NY 10012

First Regan Arts hardcover edition, July 2015.

Library of Congress Control Number: 2014955551

ISBN 978-1-941393-29-1

Interior design by Laura Klynstra
Jacket and Cover design by Richard Ljoenes
Jacket art by Archive Holdings Inc. / Getty Images

Printed in the United States of America

10   9   8   7   6   5   4   3   2   1

SO LONG AS I PERCEIVE THE WORLD AS HOSTILE,

I REMAIN LINKED TO IT: *I AM NOT CRAZY.*

—ROLAND BARTHES, *A LOVER'S DISCOURSE*

CHAPTER ONE

CHERYL

WHEN JEFFREY'S FIRST WIFE told me he had a voracious appetite for women, I assumed she was just trying to be vindictive. Now, as I walked up and down the beach on my insomnia prowl, I tried not to think about all the things he had loved about her. The list seemed short to me, but it was always long to him. Why couldn't you love her like that when she was around? I had asked once. He had no idea where the love had gone then, but it was revived after she died. Perhaps that was when I should have left, but I kept hoping we could get back to the before-time—when we felt lucky to be near each other. On mornings like this the sunrise would come up over the Long Island Sound and the neighborhood streets would be quiet and empty. Each beach house had an incredible view of the winding Connecticut shoreline, and if you squinted, you could see Long Island in the distance. Four a.m. would hit and I would find myself walking by windows trying to see what everyone was up to, hoping to see a blue wash of TV screens and peering around for something indecent. But the houses would be dark and quiet, everyone long asleep. It was the kind of neighborhood that was full of children, their soccer balls and plastic bats lingering in the streets, toy trucks lost in the manicured lawns of American flag-adorned clapboard homes. I looked down at a dirt-caked Barbie doll with kite string wrapped around her plastic arms and wondered if all these children were destined to become troubled teenagers who were shipped off to college with a sigh of relief, as we had done with Jeffrey's son, Teddy, three years before.

Without people, Little Neck Cove was one of the most breathtaking places I'd ever seen. I'd ignore the No Trespassing signs and climb down neighbors' stairs onto their beaches to walk and unwind before Jeffrey woke up. I'd pace the rocks and the beach, looking for shells, mating horseshoe crabs, or seagulls floating through the dawn sky. The beach was covered in smooth, flat stones, hidden quartz and oddly shaped blood-stones. I'd pick them up and inspect the strangest ones, dropping them into my pocket one by one. There was always snapped pieces of seashells and kaleidoscope sea glass all for the taking. These small objects that flipped and swirled along the ribbed floor of the sea would outlast us all. The soft, small waves made a hypnotic sound that would relax me into bliss. The sky would turn gray first, then light blue and finally explode with oranges and yellows. There was nothing to obscure my view here, just sky as far as I could see. I could sit on the beach for hours, listening with my eyes closed, sometimes falling asleep completely. It was the only place I didn't feel shut in, claustrophobic, unwelcome.

Hours before the humidity became unbearable, I would watch the fishermen out on the jagged rocks that jutted out into the sound, their lines glistening in the early morning glow. I knew they had been there all night, drinking and fishing as the waves lapped around them. One, an old man with a shaggy terrier, had come every summer since I met Jeffrey. He drove a beat-up truck with a raccoon tail on the antenna. Seeing him always meant the start of the summer for me. Lately, though, there were more men wandering around than usual. There was talk that we had made some online list for the best place to clam and fish. People were angry at the intrusion.

We were far away enough from New York to feel like we were in a different world, but close enough to have successful commuter husbands. In the evenings, I'd see a row of pursed-lipped wives idling their cars in the parking lot of the commuter rail station, watching their bar-car-riding husbands stagger off the train. The Connecticut shoreline was full of small towns like ours, each with an old Congregational church and a large town green at its center. Homes with plaques stating their Revolutionary age stood next to tasteful shops and cafés along Main Street. And along the water were hidden coves and snug blocks of beachside cottages. People from New York would grab them as soon as they came on the market, trying to turn this swath of Connecticut into the Vineyard or the Cape.

I passed the anchor of our little neighborhood, the Little Neck Cove Yacht & Country Club, just as the grinding daily cacophony of lawn mowers began. The decorations from last night's Gatsby party were still up. Jeffrey and I had always gone when we first got together—looking silly in a seersucker suit and a flapper dress, but it was fun. We hadn't gone in years. That's what happens: tiny adjustments and contractions to your needs because things are fun and you believe they will never stop being that way. We used to go to all the themed parties and find ourselves making out on the beach, my dress all sparkly in the moonlight. We didn't care who saw us then. We had always been the last couple dancing, full of life, our hands all over each other, sweat beading everywhere. Now I had to stanch the flow of happy memories to survive our current state of indifference toward each other. If I brushed against him, he seemed startled. I had taken the laughing and groping and desire that seemed endless for granted.

After I watched the sun rise this particular morning, I didn't feel like sneaking back into my bed, pretending I was waking up alongside

Jeffrey. He didn't appreciate my attempts at normalcy and never asked where I had been when he woke up to an empty bed anyway. It was as if he was somehow grateful for my absence.

I decided to keep walking to the neighborhood's nature trail. Built into the saltwater marshland of tall cattails, the trail traversed inlets and thick labyrinthine channels connected to the next hidden cove of homes. It was Connecticut postcard-perfect here, full of painted turtles and tiny crabs and unexpected sprays of beach roses. Whenever the tall grass was flattened back after a storm, I could see the teenager-forged trails into the hidden parts of the marsh. I'd follow the trails until they led me into a small grove with beer cans and burned-out wood piles. I'd collect the cans and clean off the wax from tree stumps, trying to erase the damage created by the late-night parties. I wanted to find them in midswing during one of my walks, see who was lusting after whom, feel what it was like to be young again, nervous and hopeful, but I only ever found the remnants of their drunken joy.

I was enjoying the bright sparkle of the water, training my binoculars on the hatching birds' nest beds staked high above the sea grass. The hiss of locusts and summer beetles filled the air, a clucking that I missed all winter long. As the sun rose, the humidity felt like a bath and I was already soaked through my shirt. I had a thin, small bird book that Jeffrey had given me in my back pocket. Now was the time when the plover birthings were in full swing and it was exhilarating. Their call notes, plaintive, bell-like whistles, filled the air around me. It was a sound unlike any other and I preferred it to humans talking. The whistles flitting around me made me feel calm yet alive. These birds were unencumbered. They just lived and flew, and most of all, they didn't betray. I tried to follow their calls and considered going off the bridge to walk along the shore, a no-no in the bird-sanctuary rule book. I wanted a closer look, so I looped one leg over the rope of the boardwalk and looked around to make sure no one was watching. Then I heard a moan, almost a groan really, and looked down. Three feet below me were two legs with sneakers and an arm feverishly moving. I pulled my leg up and backed away from the edge of the boardwalk, not wanting to disturb anything. I didn't want to be caught watching. I didn't want a confrontation.

As I hurried down the path, away from the legs, I kept turning around to make sure he wasn't following me. Who was it? A teenager? Someone's husband who liked to get off on the rocks? Finally something had happened to wake up my summer.

I looked at my watch and realized I wouldn't be able to go home and change before the club's summer fashion show. As I ran down the trail, fluffing my hair and hoping the bags under my eyes weren't too drawn, I stopped once more to see if the legs were still splayed out in the sand and rocks. They were gone. As I saw wide bird wings fill the sky, I knew the man under the boardwalk was coming. He was somewhere I couldn't see, so I ran.

At the club, I eyed the women. Could it have been one of their husbands under the bridge? Hadn't he been worried a kayaker might paddle by? I looked around, wondering what everyone's secret could be. I knew it hadn't been Jeffrey; the ankles hadn't been delicate like his. I looked at the ladies and they were all in some form of undress. We were all exposing ourselves to one another as we got ready for the runway, some more shy about it than others. Jeffrey and I hadn't had sex in two hundred and twenty-five days, but I wasn't sure if that was a lot to anyone else because it wasn't something any of us talked about. We said things like "Oh, we don't do that anymore, ha ha." But then you looked around at one another suspiciously to see who had the downcast eyes, the ones who also didn't do it anymore. At all. I wanted to know which of these women were still having sex with their husbands. I wanted to know if I was pathetic or if this was just how it turned out for everybody.

When I was a teenager, my mother used to say, "Men only love you when you're fertile, even if they don't want you to have their child." She'd looked at me, sixteen and glowing, and said, "They only want you. They want to suck out your youth. I don't have any more to give." I'd told her that it wasn't true, that men came around for her all the time, but she'd just said, "That isn't love." I'd had no view of the future, no idea she was wise.

I really shouldn't be the one with the downcast eyes. In this club, I was young. At forty-four, I had floated through the young-mother years without cesarean scars or crumpled, crepe-paper-belly skin. I had retained my figure and it had to count for something. I was the new guard. It didn't matter that Jeffrey was part of the old guard. His first wife had had to deal with key parties and rushing Teddy to bed before starting the arguments about strands of hair in the bed sheets that did not match her shade of dye. I was lucky to have missed all that. It must have troubled her, seeing Jeffrey saunter off with Johnson Picard's wife from down the block, if the rumors were true. It's one thing to hear about it and another to see it with your own eyes and not be able to do anything because you had agreed to it ahead of time. The women wad-dling around drinking Chardonnay with ice cubes, women with deep creases in the vees of their cleavage—he had slept with them first. In their white sneakers and print shirts and those . . . cotton short pants.

We were now transitioning between desirable and undesirable—that sad moment when a woman realizes that absolutely no man is looking at her, not even a passing glance. It made us all paralyzed with fear.

We battled the decline with bright, exotic colors and bold prints—anything to draw that attention back to the curves of our bodies. Even if various parts had begun to hang or droop, at least men were still looking. Men were easy after all, weren't they? Quick glances at erect

nipples under the smooth cotton of a pale pink golf shirt or at the hem
of a too-short pleated tennis skirt that seemed to elongate even the
stubbiest of lady legs. It had to cause some kind of stirring in them.
We all hoped, at least. The Shop Till You Drop fashion show had
been organized by Mary Ann to highlight the fashions from the Main
Street shops. Bring the fashion to us, we begged. And they did. Sales
reps from each boutique sat in the back row and were set to take note
on who leaned in when.

There were women of all ages going through the racks of clothes,
looking for their names, and changing into the first string of outfits
for the runway. Mary Ann had picked the models from dozens of
members. Young or old, it didn't matter; they just had to be pretty and
slim, their beauty something to aspire to. I looked at the daughters of
friends shimmying out of short shorts and then at the older women
who were watching them, forlorn, and I realized we weren't ever going
to be the ones men were looking at again. They were looking at the
daughters, the ones with taut upper arms, smooth legs, and tiny bikini
bodies who flipped from stomach to back on pool loungers all day long.
I stared at them and craved their youth and their bodies. Their youth!
I would never be that young again. It was too painful to linger on and
it wasn't something we could say out loud to one another. I wanted
to go up to each young thing and tell her, This isn't infinite for you.
Women have an expiration date. But those things hadn't registered to
my youth-dumb ears, so why should it for them? I wondered who we
were allowed to steal our youth from.

I felt a tap on my shoulder as I moved through the bodies looking for
my name and turned around to see a smiling Mary Ann.

"Oh, Cheryl, there's been a mistake."

"Did my clothes get lost?" I asked, laughing.

"Well, it's just that we don't need you. We have enough people," she
said.

"Oh."

"I overbooked, thinking some people would say no. Stage fright or vacations. I guess this year everyone wants to play Victoria's Secret angel," Mary Ann said.

"Mary Ann, it's fine. I hadn't prepared my signature move anyway," I said. I wondered if she ever felt left out. If anyone ever made her feel like deadweight. Perhaps being on top for so long made her forget that it felt terrible. I smiled through it, though. If I told anyone, it would just get back to her and I'd fall even further down her golden list. I wondered if Mary Ann had the same hierarchy for her friends who wintered in retirement homes in Florida or if it was a free-for-all. We had never been invited, but I knew they all bought near one another. I shuddered at the thought of spending a retired eternity with them, but Jeffrey jokingly referred to his retirement as his "me" time and made no mention of a second home.

"I'm doing you a favor. Do you really want to be up there and judged?" she said, smiling.

I leaned in conspiratorially and said, "These ladies are vicious, aren't they?"

Mary Ann was taken aback and I knew I had said the wrong thing. "No, of course not, they're good friends," she said.

I slid behind the curtain and saw a few open spots at the round tables. Everyone looked sharp and I felt terribly underdressed in my walking clothes. I took a seat next to Christine to wait for the show to start. Christine had chopped off her sandy blond hair a few years ago. The bowl cut was favored by the older women, but she wasn't one of them yet, so it just made her look unfeminine. She really had been beautiful once, but after child number three her waist disappeared. A waiter brought me a mimosa and I asked him to stay close. The waiters were clearing plates when I realized I was starving.

"You got the boot, huh?" Christine asked.

"Oh no, they had too many girls this year."

"Sometimes I think they just do that to put people in their place. Give them hope and take it away." She motioned with her hands, nearly spilling her sweating white wineglass on me.

"I did it a few years ago," I said, trying to save face. I had been chosen once, right before Jeffrey's first wife had died and they wanted to give me a go. See if I could be one of the girls. This was just the latest attempt at putting me in my place. It had started suddenly and passively when Mary Ann had forgotten to add me to the ticket list for *Jersey Boys* a few years ago. I wandered Times Square for hours waiting for the show to finish, fingering I Love NY and Statue of Liberty snow globes and wondering if anyone I knew would appreciate one. Afterward, they wanted to have a drink and dinner to talk about the performances. Debbie Picard told me I hadn't missed much, she would have preferred shopping, but when I showed her what I had bought, the pewter-finish Statue of Liberty for me and the I Love NY T-shirt for Jeffrey, the girls all laughed. Didn't I know about Madison Avenue? they asked. The shops around Times Square were the only ones I could find. They said it was marvelous that I had never been to New York before. They really thought it was cute. I found the most inexpensive item on the menu since I had spent so much money just walking around: a fancy grilled cheese sandwich with arugula and purple tomatoes, while they all got duck and rabbit and different things I would never think to eat. They ordered wine by the bottle while I stuck with tap water.

When the bill came, Lori said, "Split it down the middle!" And we did. I didn't want to be the one shoving twenty dollars at them, saying that it was for my portion and looking cheap or, worse, poor. Jeffrey later lectured me about spending one hundred and fifty dollars on a sandwich, and that had been my first and last visit to the city. I threw the gifts away before he could see how foolish I had been.

"I did it last year and it was a disaster. My clothes were two sizes too small and I could feel everyone's eyes on me. I still had to walk, though. They don't choose you again if you run into trouble," Christine said.

"It just seemed like a scheduling thing, that's all."

"Of course. It's not you," Christine said, patting my leg.

The models started down the makeshift runway and all the women started oohing and aahing at their friends, daughters of members, bridge partners, and golf-foursome girls. The fashion was coming to us, even if it was just from the downtown shops and featured the usual gauzy linen capris with hidden elastic waists, the tropical-colored knit separates accessorized with chunky necklaces, and the latest golf trends. They were starting with the golf fashions with breathable fabrics and I watched the models spinning and twirling in sherbet skorts. Some of them were really hamming it up.

"'Look at Karen in her divine melon skort and athletic shell. Ladies, throw a cardigan over this look and you'll be ready to go from golf course to main course in minutes,'" Mary Ann said, reading from a card.

There was clapping and laughter.

"Look at that gorgeous skirt," Christine said. "Like I need another one."

"I think Mary Ann said skort, but it'd look good on you," I said. "Treat yourself."

"Not with my hips. You, you have no hips, that would work on you."

I looked at Karen as she took a fake swing with a tiny crook in her knees, illustrating the breathability of the fabric, and wondered if that shade of melon would make me look revived.

On their return, the parade of women raised their arms as if they were winners in some unspoken competition. They had been picked. They were models all of a sudden. The rest of us guzzled mimosas and fresh midmorning sangrias and filled out forms specifying what fashions we wanted to buy.

"These things really wear me out. All the fun. I need a nap and a benzo."

"I don't think they're called that anymore," I said.

"Whatever Larry calls them, I need one."

"Maybe you shouldn't mix alcohol with them," I said.

"Oh, I do it all the time. They just have to say that. For the kids."

Christine found what she was looking for at the bottom of her purse. Her husband was a doctor who medicated her so that she'd turn a blind eye to his side projects. We all knew it but didn't say anything. No one took Christine's hand and asked her if she was okay, we always just smiled politely and ignored her confused ramblings when we realized the dose for the day was too high. Although we were complicit in her humiliation, we were all very concerned with ignoring our own.

"Bunny, everybody!"

Bunny Fogherty, nearing seventy-five, walked with purpose, with long strides and an exaggerated head toss, as if she was born for this. Big chunky jewels glittered around her neck. The other models who came through all wore an enormous amount of dazzling costume jewelry, because they knew we needed to find a way to adorn ourselves while covering the crinkle of neck skin, the dotting of sun spots on our décolletage. They led with sparkle and the tables of women were awed. "I think Bunny's found her new calling," Mary Ann said. "'This dress is straight from the Paris runways to you, ladies. Just because we live on the shoreline doesn't mean we can't be high fashion from time to time.'"

She smiled, looking up from her card.

I saw someone with scraggly hair wander through the bodies of waiting women and walk up to one of the waiters holding a tray of drinks. He peered around, confused, and I saw that it was Teddy and inhaled sharply. He was disheveled, glassy-eyed, and he was trying to get a drink off the tray as the waiter whooshed it away from him. I think I heard him say *It's for them*. Teddy actually had the nerve to wink at a newer club member as she strutted by wearing a caftan poncho thing for rainy summer evenings.

"'You never know when you're going to get wet,'" Mary Ann breathed into the microphone.

What was he doing here? I waved to get his attention and instantly regretted it when I saw him barging his way through the pushed-together chairs to walk toward me.

"Yo, Cheryl. What the hell is this?"

All the other women turned around, and I thought I felt Christine grasp my hand in support. He sat down next to me and the women stared. He was wearing jeans.

"You guys are throwing fashion shows now?"

"It's our own little Milan!" Christine said.

"You know you can't wear jeans in the clubhouse," I said.

"I'm locked out of the house."

"Does your father know you're home from school?" I asked.

Teddy laughed and said, "Nah. Who doesn't like surprises?"

He leaned back in his chair and spread his legs wide as he watched the models go by. Everyone looked away and furiously scribbled their choices on the order forms.

"Is that Mrs. Picard?" Teddy whispered. I looked to where he was looking, which was at Debbie Picard, who was sending air kisses hurtling through the air. I was embarrassed for us all.

"That's pretty good," he continued.

We had paid the summer rent on his apartment in Dartmouth in full. What was he doing here?

"Are you just visiting?" I asked.

"I got kicked out. Do you have a key to the house?"

"What do you mean, kicked out?"

"Can you believe I don't even have the key to my own house?" he asked Christine, smiling. I was mortified.

"It was a temporary thing," I assured her.

"Revoked privileges," he said.

We weren't running a prison. He just could not be trusted at home when we weren't there. I fumbled in my purse and then closed it. I started to tell him that the key was under the seashell near the front door and he got up before I could finish the rest.

Christine held my hand tightly and said, "It's okay," as if she knew what we were dealing with.

"See you at home, Cheryl. What's for dinner?"

"The club, I guess. I hadn't planned—"

"I'll find pants," he said and nearly knocked someone over trying to leave.

I looked around at the ladies and Christine said, "What a nice surprise!"

It wasn't a nice surprise at all.

The models were standing around, waiting for their drinks as the sales reps from the various boutiques started infiltrating the crowd. Everyone was pulling out credit cards and eyeing each other's selections. The whole process would take forever. I considered giving up on buying a new tennis skirt, but Christine said I absolutely could not leave without ordering one. It almost seemed like she was working on commission with the young, hungry girls.

I needed to go find Teddy.

CHAPTER TWO

TEDDY

LITTLE NECK COVE WAS an only-good-in-summer place. The streets were too narrow for cars, but drivers always tried it anyway and brought down tree branches as they passed. Everyone was playing at having old money here. Grandsons of presidents, cousins of senators, doctors and salesmen. Walking through this neighborhood made me want things suddenly—a reminder about success and what it got you. I didn't have a family business to join, but there was a spot for me in a successful corporation that sold things to keep people alive. "All of this is for you if you want it," my father always said. I didn't have to be a doctor or a lawyer, too much school. But I could excel at selling. I didn't really care if that pacemaker saved your ass; I just got off on getting people to listen to me and trust me.

Things had changed for me at school, though. They didn't want me around at their parties anymore and I was suddenly known for having bad drugs—too cut with under-the-sink garbage. I was just aggressively pursuing my natural entrepreneurial skills for pre-MBA practice, I wanted to tell them. But I got the boot anyway, reasons kept quiet, thankfully. There was no need to add further stress on my poor father's heart. They kept it simple—I had missed too many classes. It sucked to know that no one gave a shit that I was leaving. No one was crying at my door or begging me to stay in my apartment, to be with them, to pretend I was still enrolled in school to keep the party going. I mean, there were people I knew still needed me. They were just preoccupied when it came time for me to leave. No one was telling sentimental stories about sophomore-year bullshit or laughing about the time I convinced the freshman guys who followed us around like puppies to slap each other until they threw up Jager. They all did the same thing. Why was I the one getting forced out? Well, fuck them. I was moving on early. I didn't need to be dwelling in a broken-down house with vomit and turds floating in the bathroom toilet. I didn't have to scrounge for burrito money, either. I was coming back to being taken care of. Laundry done. Dinner set. Lounge chairs poolside.

I could live my future state now. Isn't that what they taught you in sales? It was all about future states and stretch goals. I drove past the club and saw the last sailing group of the day pulling their boats into the water. I parked and walked along the seawall, ignoring the No Trespassing signs tacked to the concrete. Everyone around here used to make sure you knew you weren't welcome in less obvious ways, but this was a nice touch. Let's just be direct with it. You are not wanted. Stay the hell out. Especially against the punny names of the houses around here like Wander Inn or our house, Dew Drop Inn. Was Cheryl serious? No one ever came around.

I sat on the wall and watched the kids on the Sunfish boats amble around in the bay, trying to keep themselves steady and their masts from rocking right to left as they fought to catch the wind. They were already allowed to sail without a partner, the teacher nearby in a Whaler. Who was the guy they had teaching this year? He didn't even seem to be making sure they were in control of their boats. I could do better, but they didn't let club members work here. They had to keep the divisions clear and not confuse anyone about their place in the hierarchy.

Maybe that could be my career goal—sailing instructor for wealthy seven-year-olds. Somewhere else. I watched the boats shudder out of the bay and into the sound and knew they would make it through just fine. I turned and watched the older members cross the parking lot to the club and it scared me to think that these people might have had a clue once and then had just given up and started wearing khaki shorts.

This was my prodigal-son homecoming. Isn't that how it always played out? Arms out and my father saying, "We knew you were having a rough time; we're just happy to have you back."

I laughed at the thought of it, almost begged myself to believe it.

Money wasted. I didn't quite make it through. Last time they talked about final chances. I had worn them out. No one was going to say it though, they would begin acting out some family fantasy as soon as I walked through the door and they would talk about the things I would do instead—plans and goals. I was hoping for this outcome. I really, really was. I wanted to hear all the ways I could still be successful. I wanted to know that these things happen.

I walked toward our house and at the door the key was under the seashell just as Cheryl had said. The tail of metal was sticking out. Anyone could have seen it and walked right in. There was such a sense of trust in this neighborhood. I didn't get it. A couple years ago we went rifling through summer houses in the middle of winter. We'd find the hidden keys and party all night long, wandering around strangers' houses looking at their family photos, eating whatever snacks were left-over from their stay. We thought they were probably in Florida wearing visors, floating out into the ocean, and it'd be months before they found clogged toilets, puke-lined beds, and empty booze cabinets.

Cheryl was just asking to become a statistic. Not that they ever went anywhere and I had no idea when my dad was planning on retiring or if he'd even be taking Cheryl with him. But still. I didn't want people going through their stuff.

Inside, the house was dead quiet. All the windows were closed like we didn't live at the beach. I opened the refrigerator and found nothing but boxed salad and a couple tomatoes and a carton of half-and-half. Some questionable leftovers in Tupperware. She was really falling down on the job here. The freezer was even sadder. A wall of Tupperware filled with fucking chicken soup as if she was stockpiling for the apocalypse. I got a box of Triscuits from the cabinet and took my stuff upstairs. I don't know why Cheryl insisted on showcasing shit from high school around my room. Old lacrosse sticks on the wall and yearbooks fanned out on my desk like it was a fucking coffee table. I was going to have to talk to her about coming into my room when I wasn't home, again. I put my bags in the corner; I'd go back for the boxes in my trunk later. You know, start small, and ease into this. I looked through my stuff and couldn't find any weed. This was unacceptable. I had put it in one of my bags last night and now it was gone. Someone must have gone through them while I was asleep to get their rent money or whatever. I went through my drawers because I knew I had a stash somewhere, even if it was super stale. Maybe I could talk Cheryl into letting me have space in the freezer for my unmentionables. I laughed just thinking about it. Put your frozen peas over here and I'll put my eighths over there, Cheryl.

My room came up with nada. Now I was gonna have to stress about finding someone to get weed from. Who was even still around? Probably fucking Steven, and I hated doing business with him. I could do a trade—my bad shit for his twigs and sticks. Or Pauline. Pauline would give me anything I wanted.

I headed to my dad and Cheryl's room. I was nervous about what I'd find in there. Spent K-Y Jelly squeeze tubes? I doubted it, actually.

I hadn't found one of those in a long time and I hadn't even seen them even touch each other in years. I pulled open my dad's bedside table and looked through the pill bottles to find something I could munch on. Heart medicine, arthritis medicine, blister pack of Viagra. I thought about grabbing some for later, because why not, but I checked the expiration date and they were dunzo two years ago. Damn, nothing more depressing than expired Viagra. I put it back where I found it and went through the rest of the bottles.

And there, like a beautiful light, was a half-full bottle of oxycodone. I opened it and my chalky white heaven poured out. Thank you, Dad. Thank you and your fucked-up arthritis. I love you so much. I took a few and figured I'd steal more as needed, or until he figured it out and hid them. All those low-voiced commercials of dread, commanding parents to keep their pills locked away from their children, hadn't scared him into hiding them from me.

I took the pills back to my room and crushed one on my desk and snorted it real tight. It was just gonna be a little bit to tide me over because the Vicodin wasn't doing shit. I went to take a shower because nothing feels better when you're high than hot water. It's like you can imagine standing under a warm waterfall and there's a numb buzz in your head and maybe it's like being inside something bigger than you. Maybe, like, I don't know, a vat of warm honey. Just soft. I left my clothes in a pile, turned on the shower, and waited for the big mirrors to steam up.

I looked at myself and thought, This is you, Teddy. This is all about second chances, right, brother? You're on a game show and this is you getting your shit together. I made fierce faces at myself in the mirror to show that I meant it. The numb buzzing was hitting hard and I went into the shower, closed the glass door, and stood under the water. I opened my mouth to let it all in. I wanted to drown in it.

CHAPTER THREE

CHERYL

I PASSED THE TENNIS COURTS and listened to the pop of tennis balls hitting racquets—percussive pop pop pops as tanned arms swung back and
forth in perfect unison—and followed the one-way road back toward
the water and my home. At the Hughes' house—"Bay Hoovs Us"—
Lori was bent over picking out weeds from around the Petite Lizette
heirloom roses she had strategically placed all around the perimeter. I
was surprised she wasn't ordering her gardeners to do it.

"Oh, Cheryl!" Lori shouted.

I waved hello and took note of her new personalized license plate—
LOVE 40. Her obsession with tennis was unparalleled in this neighborhood. Despite that, she was short and round and always seemed
unhappy. Once she even confided in me that she was lonely. Who
wasn't? Her husband was a partner at a top New York law firm. What
more could she want or need? I tried to extricate myself, worried about
what Teddy was doing in the house, but she was not interested in letting me go.

"Why weren't you at the fashion show?" I asked.

"I went to the VIP preorder."

I didn't even know about the VIP preorder.

"Hey, Mrs. Hughes, do you still need me to watch your dogs this weekend?"

We both turned around and saw Steven walking toward us. Lori seemed taken off guard. She said, "Didn't your mother give you the message? We aren't going away after all."

I sometimes played doubles opposite his mother. He was handsome with deep-set eyes and thick dark hair. I lingered too long looking at his muscular arms and broad shoulders and he kept his eyes on me long enough for it to be noticeable. I blushed at the attention. He was a child, really, even if he didn't look it.

"That sucks." He looked at me, momentarily embarrassed, then said, "Sorry." He smiled and asked: "How are you doing, Mrs. Willard?"

"Fine. Fine. Are you working this summer?" I asked.

"Nah. Taking the summer off. Hey, you take any pictures of those sunrises you watch?"

"No," I said, startled that he knew I was pacing the streets each dawn.

"Too bad. I bet you'd get some great ones." He said good-bye and walked away.

Lori gave me a look. "What was that about?" she asked.

"Sometimes I get up early and take a walk. I didn't think anyone was paying attention," I said, watching him go. I'd never seen him on the street before and I wondered when he'd seen me. Who else watched me pacing the streets under the lamplights?

"Don't hire him to do anything because he'll rob you blind," Lori said. "He ate all the cookies in my pantry. Crackers, too. I bet he had a party."

"They all do," I said.

"Some are worse than others. And he's one you have to watch out for.

Do you know they had to pull him out of school? For good this time."

"College is hard, Lori. I didn't have an easy time of it, either."

"Apparently, he was having 'issues.' I wonder how Fran's going to whitewash this episode."

Steven's mother, Fran, had become increasingly protective of him. He used to wander at low tide for hours looking for oysters to sell around the neighborhood, smart and entrepreneurial from the get-go. He was the kind of son you wanted to have because he was going to be someone special. Except something had happened and he stopped getting things right. His deviancy was overlooked at first, but it had been snowballing lately. He had locked two seagulls in his mother's bathroom last summer, and when she came home, they attacked her—squawking and shitting everywhere. She ran out of the house screaming and the birds followed her out the front door. I chuckled thinking about it—Fran's own starring role in *The Birds*.

"The school saw him as a threat," Lori whispered. I asked her to whom, but she had no answer. I knew she had heard it thirdhand.

"He also went through my closets."

"Maybe he just wanted to see how he looked in your tennis skirts. I'm sure he has nice legs."

"As if you need more men in your life when you've got Jeffrey."

I was always hearing these indictments from women around here, but they had no idea. I had resigned myself to nodding politely and pretending I was ravaged nightly or at least weekly. Once I even heard someone say, I wouldn't mind having his slippers under my bed. I wanted to shout at them all, tell them the truth, but what could I say? There was no need to embarrass myself in front of them. They wouldn't show me any kindness about it; it would just become drunken dinner-party conversation to make themselves feel better. It would start with, *Can you believe after all that they don't even screw? How sad*, they would say in unison. *How sad is she?* I didn't need their pity, so I kept it to myself. Except sometimes, looking around, I wanted to tell someone and not hear *This was your choice.*

"I'm not saying I'm going to do anything with him, Lori. I'm saying he's handsome."

"You're terrible," she said, laughing.

She watched him disappear around the bend and I knew what she was thinking, even if she didn't want to admit it. We were both thinking it. Even if it only flitted through our minds for a moment, the shame came right after it, hard and fast. But the attention, even if just a passing glance, was thrilling and I held on to it. I stared at the bumper of her car, at the placard that said FOR GOD, FOR COUNTRY, AND FOR HARVARD, and started to inch away from her fence when she said, "I need to talk to you about your tree."

"Oh, Lori. I've been meaning to talk to Jeffrey about it," I said as I turned away quickly. But I could not shake her; she squared off in front of me, pointing at the tree that overlapped our yards.

"I don't think you understand the severity of the situation, Cheryl. The tree is dead. Another big storm and it's going to fall on my house."

It was conversations like these, the starts of conversations like these, that made me wonder why people couldn't just be happy here. Instead, I listened to endless conversations about shrubs a few inches too high, saw neighbors on alert and busily notating where dogs were defecating, devoted hours to committee meetings regulating everything, and now it was a tree with a bit of a lean. It wasn't even dead. We had checked. I had wormed my way into this neighborhood, thinking it was a place where people spent their time playing tennis and having after-golf drinks, where everyone felt lucky every day. How could you not in a place like this? Instead, Lori Hughes tried to muscle me into cutting down the one thing in my yard that had been there longer than anything else. I think it was actually protected. I didn't think we could cut it down even if we wanted to. I could have ended up somewhere less exclusive but with more varied paint hues. Even somewhere as offensive enough as to allow vinyl siding. I could have ended up somewhere where people had good reason to be unhappy. It's not as if Lori had to live next to people who were constantly adding on to their house. How many cars did one have to fit in one's garage? The incessant drilling and sawing and banging were enough to drive anyone insane.

We heard a crash and turned around and stared at our middle-aged neighbor, Tuck, teetering half off his bicycle. Khaki shorts, Top-Siders, and a fraying, faded polo shirt. He was bent over, looking at his leg, which sported a fresh cut, a trickle of blood.

"Fuck."

"Language," Lori said.

"Natural hazards," he said, smiling.

He took a sip from his beer glass that he somehow managed to hold while maneuvering his handlebars.

"Don't you start early," Lori said, looking at his drink.

Tuck said, "Don't you have a IT's 5 O'CLOCK SOMEWHERE magnet on your fridge?"

Lori shrugged and said, "Yeah, I do."

"There you go," he said. Tuck and I laughed; Lori shot me a look and I shut up.

"Beautiful day, am I right?" he said.

Tuck finished off his beer, raising the glass high as he tried to get the last drips out of the bottom. "You ladies hitting the driving range later? I could give you a ride."

"For god's sake, Tuck," Lori moaned. "We are having a conversation."

Tuck winked at me as he got back up on his bike and said, "Your loss." He pedaled away, glass in hand.

"He thinks because someone in his family was the president he can do whatever he wants," Lori said.

Maybe it had been Tuck under that bridge.

Lori cut through my daydreaming and said, "You'll be liable for any property damage, Cheryl. I don't want to have to do that to you."

She made a face of grave concern, like she really was looking out for my best interest. We were living in a presidential neighborhood, and even if the lineage had been corrupted with boozing and laziness, everything had to look exactly so.

"I'll have Jeffrey take another look," I said and started walking away, hoping to diffuse the situation. She kept following me and I stopped at the edge of her fence next to a big yellow sign illustrated with a dog in motion with snarling teeth and the words MY DOG DOESN'T LIKE STRANGERS in bold black letters. It seemed unnecessary for this neighborhood; who would be skulking in the yards here? The association paid to have a guard drive around in his little Dodge Neon every night, so there was no need to advertise the fact that her dogs were assholes.

"Don't you think things like this create disharmony in the neighborhood?" I asked, pointing at her sign. I wanted her to feel like she was doing something a little bit wrong.

We heard whistling and she looked past me and said, "Oh God."

I turned around and saw a man peeing in between two cars, right on the road. He was a fisherman, a white bucket and a pole next to him. He finished, zipped up, and looked at us like he wanted something from us or just wanted us. He had the kind of tan you get from sleeping outside. Lori moved closer to me. "Don't look scared," she whispered as I tried to act normally. We narrowed our eyes at him, unified. I searched for Tuck but didn't see him or his bicycle anywhere. He was probably refilling his beer or antagonizing children by the club. Lori started getting closer to me again and I got nervous.

"Who do you think you are? You can't just do that here!" I said, trying to be courageous and mean.

The urinator looked at us and mumbled something in Spanish. Lori pulled still closer to me and whispered something I couldn't hear.

"What?"

"He's Mexican," she said. "We have to do something." Lori shouted at the man. "You are not allowed to walk on my beach. You shouldn't be out there!"

What did she mean by "my beach," anyway?

"You better leave right now! I have dogs!" she yelled loudly.

I stared back at her sign—the snarling dog in midflight. I was curious if she'd leave me on the street to let the dogs out to chase him. But I knew they wouldn't even get out of the yard because they had those collars that Tasered them if they stepped outside of the invisible line. I looked around and didn't hear any leaf blowers or mowers and I realized that we were probably alone on the street, us against him. Lori ran through the gate into her yard and slammed it behind her, jamming her finger deep into the latch and yelping loudly. The man and I were both startled as Lori clutched her hand. I was surprised by my fear. He was just a fisherman, after all.

"My finger!" she said. She looked at the man and snarled at him, "It's your fault!"

Lori was taking it upon herself to square off with him, but I had had enough and told her, "Let's go."

"Where are you going?" Lori said with indignation. She launched out of her yard and trailed after me, cradling her finger, as the man stood in the street, unmoving.

"I'm going to go get help," I said.

"Don't leave me behind," Lori said, worried.

"Are you okay?" I asked, trying to get a look at her finger.

"I'm hurt pretty bad," she said. I looked down at her shaking hand. The finger was swollen and turning purple.

"*Gringas*," he said, shaking his head.

I turned to Lori, who looked terrified.

"What does it mean?" she asked.

"White women," I said matter-of-factly.

"Who does he think he is?"

I started walking toward my house with my arm around her for sup-port and she whispered that we had to call the police. I ignored her at first, but then she convinced me. She said that this could be the begin-ning of an escalation of violence.

My front door was nearly wide open and at first we were afraid to go inside.

"He broke in," Lori whispered.

I looked around and saw that the seashell where I hid the house key was overturned and figured it must have been Teddy.

I pushed in and called "Hello!" while Lori stared out into the street at the fisherman. There was no answer and I went to call the police as Lori locked the door, closing us in together. I looked around and didn't see a sign of Teddy. He wasn't in the backyard, either.

"Who are you screaming for? You think robbers are going to respond?" she asked.

"It's just Teddy."

"This guy knows where you live now. We should have gone some-where else," she said.

Lori was acting like we were in our own episode of *Dateline*. She was always coaxing us to discuss if we thought our husbands were the mur-dering kind. If our net worths were worth it. On last Friday's episode, a woman had vanished from her home—"without a trace," Lori kept saying. We all had our theories because we all watched the show, but Lori was the loudest. It was the husband. It was always the husband. I wondered if she walked around worrying that her own was trying to snuff her out. Their net worth was worth it.

I could see the wheels in her mind rolling, readying herself for her TV interview, saying things like "We used to be an all-doors-unlocked community."

"We should have snuck around the beach way to lose him," I said, imagining my own version of the story.

"What a disaster," she said.

"Nine one one, what's your emergency?"

"Hello, I'd like to report a suspicious man in Little Neck Cove. He's carrying a fishing pole and a bucket. He was urinating in the street. Yes, public urination."

I stared at Lori, who was hunched over and peeking through my curtains, and realized that I had never let her in my house before. I looked around and saw that there was dust on the plants, things in disarray.

Lori came away from the window and started looking around, inspecting things.

"He drove off," she said.

"He drove off," I said into the phone.

The dispatcher asked me if we saw the car and I asked Lori and she said it was white, maybe a hatchback, "a shitty little car," she called it. "That's how you know he didn't belong," she added. To Lori, being poor meant desperation; it meant being a criminal. I had driven a "shitty little car" for half my life until I met Jeffrey. I remember the first time I got into his luxury sedan, how roomy it was. There were no crumbs anywhere. The polished wood on the steering wheel gleamed. The leather was soft on my bare legs. I had never felt leather so soft. I couldn't believe they made cars like that. I had tried to sew the worn-down seat-cover seams in my own car many times, but they just kept splitting open, showing the yellowing liner underneath. The first time Jeffrey rode in my car, I could feel the heat coming off my face as he looked at the radio with the broken tape player and when he tried the passenger-side window that only I could roll down and reached for the broken-off door light I had in my center console. Asking, "What's this?" When I tried to explain, it still didn't make sense to him. *How did someone not fix the short in their door light? What do you mean it would run out the battery? These things can be fixed.* These were the things I imagined him saying to me, or perhaps, even, *Why do you have so many clothes littering the backseat?*, while eyeing the work shirts and weekend-wear from overnight stays. I worried he'd say it looked like a hoarder's car. Instead he said, "I'll pamper you."

We had met when I was working as the assistant manager of the men's department at the Ralph Lauren store at the outlet mall off I-95. He had come in, bashful and cute, needing new dress shirts for work. I had never dated a customer before, but he was persistent. It had taken him months to work up the courage and then he wouldn't let up until I said I'd have coffee with him. I told him it would have to be the food court because my breaks were short. After that, things went quickly.

"He left beer cans on the street! Extra-large ones."

I told the dispatcher and hung up the phone as Lori stopped in front of the splatters.

"I was going to clean that."

"It's so difficult sometimes," she said, clucking her tongue. She stared out at the rocks, at the fishermen sitting far out there. It still felt impossible that something like this could be mine, even secondhand.

"How can you stand them?" she asked.

"Who?"

"All those strange men sitting out there. I'd be so scared."

She had lived in tiny towns, no-name places, married well, and ended up here. She made no secret of it. Everyone was a threat to the life she cultivated in this beach community. I stared out and watched the men fishing. They lived somewhere the highway led you to, away from here, somewhere women like Lori never ventured to. Her farthest trip was circling the crowded parking lots of warehouse-size grocery stores at the edge of town. The only news coming from the outside world lived on her television set with frequent reenactments of medium-size city gun battles that kept her and everyone else here huddled in their community.

"It's disgusting," she said. "When they need to use the restroom, they just go out there. They pee in the ocean. They do other things in the ocean, too."

"I think it's been established that peeing in the ocean is okay. Other stuff like what?"

"I suppose you're fine with people peeing in the street, then."

"Didn't you just see me call the police?" I asked.

"Are you really going to make me say it, Cheryl?" She waited, then said, "Susan Humphrey told me she saw them pooping from her window."

I shook my head in disbelief. She didn't even know I was faking my shock, making fun of her *just a little*. I liked to get the ladies riled up sometimes, if only to feel a part of something. A collective outrage. It was only fair after so many "lost" invitations to get-togethers or watching all the girls grab a table together by the pool with no room for me to join in. These little hurts accumulated and I tried to get back at them in the smallest, most discreet ways possible. I didn't know what else I could do to make myself fit in and I was finally tired of trying. Worn out, exhausted. Done in. Some people here looked like they just casually rolled out of bed every morning and got on the golf course, but I pressed my clothes, I made sure my hair always had a shine, I did the things that I learned over time were absolutely necessary here for me. When Mary Ann said orange was unflattering, I listened and threw out anything with an overly citrus feel. When Lori exclaimed that everyone had to take Pilates with the visiting instructor, Beth, or they truly didn't *get it*, I did it. Yet it almost felt like the one time they had asked me to walk at the fashion show, it was out of pity. I had really given it my all. I had learned moves, I had practiced in front of Jeffrey, and I had even taken his suggestions. To not be asked back year after year was embarrassing. Now to pretend I was up for it and then snub me, well, it had taken all I had left. Jeffrey always said that if he saw my potential, they had to, too. He said it over and over again like it must be true, until he got tired of saying it. Maybe he stopped seeing my potential, too. Maybe I had been a bad bet all along. Why I still cared, I don't know.

I stared at Lori's big, watery eyes and knew I wanted to be her neighbor forever, no matter what nonsense came streaming out of her mouth. I had nowhere else to go.

"My children swim in that water," she said. "No one should use the ocean as their restroom."

Yes, I understood what she was saying, that I would never be able to comprehend what it felt like to have my own children swim in a sea full of feces. She was right. I only had a stepson and the idea of Teddy doing laps in a cesspool only made me feel slightly bad. And right now, if he was passed out upstairs, not bad at all.

"There's a lot of pollution out there, with the boats and all," I said.

"Clearly that's a different situation. They belong here. Those people don't belong here. Look what that man was doing. What he almost did to us. He could take it a step further and attack someone," she said.

"We can build a fence, gate up the community," I said, joking.

"You're so right, Cheryl. A gate would raise property values, anyhow. You know what? I'm going to call a special meeting with the association. We have to get the dangerous element out of here. Think about the children."

Everyone was always thinking about children. She looked at me with pity in her eyes because I was never thinking about the children, and that was a problem.

"We can think about it a little while before we call a meeting, maybe," I said.

"The time to act is now. Before something happens, not after."

"I don't want anything to happen to any child, that's for sure," I said. "But maybe they're just enjoying the summer."

"Don't be absurd," Lori said.

I went back to the window. I stared at a family making their way onto the rocks. The father carried a white bucket, his two small children carried petite fishing poles, and they didn't look dangerous at all. He just looked like he was trying to show his family something nice.

I called for Teddy again and got no answer.

"I should really go check on him," I said.

She smiled and said, "What a nice surprise to have him here."

"I'll be right back," I told her and walked up the stairs, feeling the doom of potentially finding an intruder, or something wrong with Teddy, and having to face Lori if she was still sitting in the kitchen when I came back down. Teddy's door was ajar and I peered in and saw him sleeping naked on top of his bed. I hadn't even had a chance to put sheets on. I closed the door as quickly as I could in case, god forbid, Lori had followed me up the stairs. I heard the door close as I walked down the stairs. I walked over to the window and saw her talking animatedly with Jeffrey, her swollen finger waving through the sky, his eyes following it. She went and picked up a can from where the man had dropped them and started waving that around, too. I could see her vigilante spirit awakening right then.

"Teddy's naked and passed out upstairs," I said as Jeffrey walked in the door. He had a thing about not hitting him with anything upsetting when he got home from work, but this was worth noting.

"What are you talking about?"

He looked back down at the mail, at the J. Jill and Eddie Bauer catalogs he was holding, and sighed.

I said, "I think it's permanent."

He stopped at a tattered envelope and pushed it my way, saying, "This one is returned mail for you. Who lives in Killingly?"

I stared at the letter, my handwriting, with a big red stamp demanding it be returned to the sender right there.

My mother. I should have never included my return address on my check for this very reason. I didn't answer him; instead I just shrugged my shoulders.

"Are you going to check to see if he's breathing?" I asked.

Jeffrey glared at me and asked what time he had gotten in.

"I don't know what time he got in, but he was begging for drinks at the fashion show and then left the front door wide open like it was no big deal." I walked toward Jeffrey. "I think this time it's permanent."

"I heard you the first time," he said. "I'm sure he'll be hungry when he wakes up. Do we have anything?"

I pointed to the freezer so that Jeffrey would get the picture and he did because he said maybe the club was a better idea. He climbed the stairs to go greet Teddy and I ripped open the letter with shaking hands, expecting to find something besides what I had sent to her myself—a personal check for one thousand dollars, just like every month. She had told me about a reverse mortgage gone wrong before we stopped speaking. I didn't want her to be kicked out of the only place she still had. It was as much as I could squirrel away each month to send to her from what Jeffrey gave me. I stared at the check and the abrupt line on a grocery note: Hope you are well. Not even my name signed on the note because it was on the check, and why be redundant?

What was she trying to tell me? To stay out of her business? I was doing what I thought a daughter should do, a gentle nudge to let her know someone was still looking out for her. When I first got together with Jeffrey, she started almost immediately. Her windows needed to be replaced. The water heater was twenty years old and also needed to be replaced. My sisters were next—their children needed so many things. At first Jeffrey was kind, but it was always embarrassing. I half expected them to move in with us, tell him we were a package deal. I went to my mother's house to give her money and found that the windows still had their rotten wooden frames. Nothing had been fixed. She wouldn't tell me what she was doing with the money we gave her. She said I owed her for all the years she had given up for me. My mistake had been to tell Jeffrey, who said he was done bankrolling all of them. I had to let go of the burden or I would lose him. Who would choose the sad trap of where they came from over the dream life that was close enough to touch?

I started sending my mother checks last year, as if that would somehow make up for the years of neglect. This one was the first returned. I thought that fixed incomes made it difficult to get the necessities in life. I was trying, but she didn't want to see me. She wouldn't answer the phone when I called. She said I had always been ungrateful. I stared at the envelope and wondered if she had even touched it. She hadn't cashed the last check and I thought it might have been some kind of message: *Stop.* She didn't need me at all.

I could hear Jeffrey and Teddy arguing upstairs.

Teddy with his eye rolls and sudden bursts of anger that later morphed into bored indifference toward us. We were morons to him, a bank that dispensed money when necessary and answered the phone to midnight-nervous calls about vague troubles. I told Jeffrey to stop giving him money, let him learn what it means to be a grown-up, but Jeffrey would not consider it until Teddy was finished with school. He had to be supported because he was Jeffrey's son. How would it look if Jeffrey didn't give him everything? It wasn't as if I had a say, anyway. It didn't matter that I had been around for almost ten years; I was still a bystander in their lives together.

I heard the rumble of footsteps and looked up. Jeffrey was staring down at me and told me to get ready to go. I told him that maybe it wasn't such a good idea. I told him I could run out and get something for us to eat. Steamers and lobsters. Or something celebratory.

"To celebrate what?" Jeffrey asked.

"I don't mean celebrate. I mean, he doesn't seem to be in the right headspace to handle a meal."

"He's just tired."

Teddy had been consistently tired or out of sorts or under the weather since we found him on the beach at age twelve, drunk and stoned. Jeffrey had many variations of ailment choices for Teddy, but the symptoms were always the same.

"I'll be ready in a few," I said. Upstairs, I passed the bathroom and heard Teddy retching in the toilet. I listened through the door and it seemed like he might have even been crying. I heard the flush and quickly made my way to the bedroom, quietly closing the door behind me. I didn't want him to know I was there and make the indignity worse.

I went to my closet and stared in. I was at a loss. The sherbet tops made me wince, but my navy dresses seemed too dour. Red was calling attention unnecessarily. What did shorts say about a person?

All of a sudden I felt like everything was coded. What did big, obnoxious polka dots say? It was too exhausting to think about. I picked a pink top with a yellow pony on it, my go-to, because it would set off my tan nicely. It also said happy and youth. Pick me next time. I had stockpiled clothes from the outlets that would last me and Jeffrey for years. I looked at myself holding the shirt up, making sure it was okay, and didn't like what I saw.

I didn't need to be picked. I grabbed a melon top that I saw buried deep and put it on. Screw Mary Ann and her anti-citrus rule.

"Cheryl, are you wearing that?" Jeffrey asked me when I went downstairs.

"Yes," I said with hesitation.

I looked down at myself. I thought the melon looked great. I applied pink lipstick with a small mirror in my purse and tried to keep busy while we waited for Teddy to come down. As I stared at my lips in the mirror, I thought that if my mother had moved, there was no way to find out where she had gone. The women in my family were all so stubborn. There would be no call to say she was relocating. No notice from my sisters. We all had run from the same home and away from one another. The only contact I'd had with my mother had been seeing the monthly withdraws from my checking account.

"Should I go check on him?" I asked.

Jeffrey screamed Teddy's name louder than I had ever heard and asked, "Was that so hard?"

"My voice doesn't carry like yours," I said. I felt like playing up my sense of fear during this afternoon's debacle with Lori. Perhaps if he felt like I was somehow fragile it would make him be nicer to me.

"Do I look okay?" I asked.

"You look fine."

"That's it? I know I'm not a model, but still."

"What is it you'd like me to say?" Jeffrey asked.

I thought for a moment and then shrugged my shoulders. "How about something a little more exciting than 'fine'?"

"All right, I liked it better when you looked vulnerable," he said. "How does that sound?"

"I think I don't like what you mean."

"If you don't, be sure about it," he said.

I looked at him as he shook his head at me, bored. He was still slim, tanned. Almost slight. He liked it better when I looked vulnerable. I let the words roll around in my head. It was hard not to count the number of days since we had last had sex or the other long pauses before. He hadn't wanted me vulnerable in all that time, but that's how he liked me best. Jeffrey looked old. I knew that. But men could be without the necessity for any nips or tucks. My mother had told me that twenty years would seem further and further apart the older we got, but I hadn't listened. She had always said that one day I would feel that certain kind of loss, of someone not needing you anymore. Once, I saw her entwined with an old man from down the street, whispering in his ear. It was a sense of intimacy that I had always strived to achieve. The way a man's face looked when my mother leaned into him. That's what I wanted. I learned the allure of secretive intimacy from her and it's what sustained me and Jeffrey in the beginning. We loved each other and couldn't keep away from each other. How could it have just floated away? I couldn't reconcile now with then, when everything seemed possible. I thought I would always feel Jeffrey's need, his want. My mother would just smirk at me as if I were more foolish than anyone she had ever known.

I saw my mother's power over men when I was a child. When they'd first come around, they were insatiable. The gifts were always best, the perfumes and lotions and fancy clothes. My sisters and I would ransack the bounty when she went out. Later, I'd channel her when I felt the need for attention. The sweet lilt in her voice transferred into mine like magic; a quick flick of my index finger along a man's broad shoulder while whispering my want always worked. These were just dates, though. Nothing permanent. I wanted to keep moving, until I found Jeffrey. Already soured by the lengths she would go to as her attractiveness waned and she aged, my mother changed her focus: it became less about the gifts men gave her and more about the necessities of living they provided for with their cash. When I met Jeffrey at thirty-four, he had made me feel that those impermanent early-on-in-the-relationship feelings could indeed be permanent, the gooseflesh rising with the simplest touch forever. I forgot that those thrilling feelings were still possible.

I smiled at Jeffrey. I poured myself some gin, threw in a few cubes, and didn't even bother to top it off with tonic. Jeffrey raised his eyebrow. I went over and rubbed his shoulder and he jumped away from me as soon as Teddy barreled down the stairs. Teddy didn't even look at us as he went to the fridge, pulled out a beer, and took a swig.

"Already starting, huh?" Jeffrey said.

"You want to do this now? I figured we'd wait until after dinner," Teddy said.

Jeffrey stared at him as I kept sipping my gin, hoping I would never reach the bottom. Jeffrey made one for himself out of anger or maybe defeat. Teddy had messy hair but was still handsome, golden-haired and fresh-faced. And I could understand that girls probably cried over him for hours, because he did not give a shit about anyone at all. I saw the older women at the club looking at him, and not as though they admired him for their daughters. They wanted him all to themselves, even at their age. Did they really think we still existed to boys his age?

"I found pants, Cheryl," Teddy said.

"Good, I'm glad."

"He was walking around without pants?" Jeffrey asked.

"No, jeans. Don't worry about it."

Jeffrey eyed us both as if we were the same. A problem for him. "Maybe you want to brush your hair," he said to Teddy.

I was sure that Jeffrey would take him to his barber and cut off the length, make him nip it to right above the ears so he could go to corporate meet-and-greets. This was just a phase, a last sigh of careless independence before it was time to be a man and follow his father. Maybe. I just hoped he would let us live in peace while the last bit of wildness seeped out of him.

Jeffrey finished off his drink and I knew that he'd be switching to scotch at dinner. It was going to be just like that all night.

Teddy pulled a rubber band from his pocket and tied his hair back. Jeffrey watched him do it and then studied him. He was taller than Jeffrey and he looked dirty and mean to me. Like the kind of men I once liked but now steered clear of.

"You look like a woman," Jeffrey said.

"What do you know?" Teddy asked.

Teddy turned to me and looked me up and down, making me instantly uncomfortable.

"What?"

"Did you buy that at the fashion show?" Teddy asked.

"No, I didn't. Why, is it bad?" I asked, looking down at myself.

He shook his head and said, "You're looking more and more like the rest of them. All you're missing is that leathery tan and a fluorescent onesie like old Elaine."

"I think I'll change."

"Don't change. Come on, I'm kidding," Teddy said, laughing.

"I'm not like them," I said. Why was I even arguing with him?

"Jesus Christ," Jeffrey said, already halfway out the door.

I drank the rest of my gin in a rush and followed Teddy out.

"I hope you aren't doing this on my account," Teddy said at the table. "I've been sick since I got here. Can't eat."

Jeffrey lowered his menu and took a large sip of scotch. I could hear Teddy's leg bouncing under the table. It was making me nervous and I wanted to put my hand on his knee to make him stop.

"Isn't that the friend you used to play golf with sitting over there?" I asked.

Teddy turned to look, then turned back quickly and said, "Nah, I wasn't his type." Jeffrey nearly spit out his scotch and I stared down at the menu with newfound fascination, trying not to laugh. There had always been rumors.

"Will you grow up?" Jeffrey said, pissed. He looked at both of us in disgust, as if he was thinking *This can't be who I ended up with.*

"Cheryl!"

I looked up and Bunny Fogherty was standing above me, wearing the all-pastel-pink number she had modeled earlier. Teddy was right: I had completely fallen for this. Her short cotton pants had bows at the pockets. I covered myself with my arms and wanted to hide.

"Bunny! I thought I saw you over there," I said. "You were marvelous today."

"Oh, stop. I'm too old to be a real model," she said, smiling and loving it. "The whole family's here. How nice!"

"Impromptu," I said.

Bunny was eyeing us all. Teddy was staring at the menu and the floor under the table nearly shook from his anxious leg bounce.

"Are you okay?" I whispered to him.

He stopped his anxious tics and focused his attention on Bunny. She pounced on him, rubbing his shoulders vigorously.

"We were wondering when we were going to see you again!" she said.

"Who's 'we'?" Teddy asked.

"All of us," Bunny said, waving her arm to reveal the crowded room of diners. "We all missed you," she continued.

"I missed you, too," Teddy said, amused.

Bunny pointed out the window at the boats bobbing in the harbor and said, "What's not to miss?" She laughed and laughed. "What do you think you'll do now? Are you out of school?" Bunny asked.

"Yeah, I'm out. The sky's the limit, really. I can do it all," Teddy said, smiling.

He had turned on the charm and it was working. Bunny clapped her hands together.

"A boy like this can do anything! That confidence is an asset!" she said. She held her hands together and stared at Teddy, who was still smiling at her with all his might.

"We are just so happy to have you back. We need a little young blood around here." She nudged me and I agreed.

"We do need some young blood to give those guys on the golf course a run for their money!" I said.

"I hate golf," Teddy said. Jeffrey wiped his brow and looked away from our table.

"You love the water," I said.

"I do, that's true," he said, staring off into space. "I do love that water. I do love to sail."

"We got it," Jeffrey said.

"Did Cheryl tell you about her near-death experience today with Lori and. . ." She trailed off and leaned in close.

She whispered, "A Mexican."

"How do you know he was Mexican?" Teddy asked.

She waved him off, adults-talking style. Jeffrey said Lori had mentioned it and I wondered what embellishments she had added.

"We're fine," I said.

"Just barely, I heard," Bunny said.

"This has been a long-term problem and I'm surprised it's just coming to a head now," Jeffrey said. "There are families setting up picnics on the rocks like they live here."

"Right. What gives them the right to enjoy it? Do they pay taxes here? No, they don't. I do," Bunny said aggressively.

"They just want to see a bit of beach. It's all private up and down the coast except for one place," I said.

"They can go there then and pay the entrance fee. Nothing's for free," Bunny said. She narrowed her eyes at me and said, "Don't you care about safety?"

"Of course I do," I told her. But everyone looked at me like I didn't care about safety, like I thought danger was no big deal.

"It sounded positively terrifying," Bunny said.

"What'd he do, touch you?" Teddy said.

Bunny inhaled sharply and Teddy started to laugh.

"He was drunk and using the street like his public toilet and he lunged at Lori and Cheryl," Bunny said.

"Lori's finger is pretty banged up," I said. "She could have really hurt herself. He didn't do it, though. She did."

"Whose side are you on, Cheryl?" Bunny said. "It's terrible to be afraid in your own neighborhood. Lori had a brilliant idea to build a fence and install a gate. We're going to do it."

"Lori's idea?" I asked.

"She's just so community-oriented. A natural leader. I could see her being president of the club one day."

"God, I hope not," Jeffrey said.

"Well, what's obvious is that we have a real problem with these people," said Bunny.

"What do you mean 'these people'?" asked Teddy, suddenly curious.

Bunny stared at Teddy and he said, "Sounds pretty racist."

"Lori said he had a knife," Bunny said, leaning in close.

I thought back. Had I seen a knife? Now I wasn't sure. Why would Lori make something like that up? He was just peeing; he had a fishing pole and a bucket. Other women started coming toward the table.

"Are you okay?" they all asked at once.

"It's been a long day," I answered.

Bunny stared straight at me and asked me if I had been scared.

"We all know Lori's not much help," I said. The women didn't appreciate my sense of humor, so I said, "It just felt uncomfortable." They were salivating for details. They wanted mayhem.

Leslie, who I usually like very much, looked at me as if I was lying.

"I was only scared in the moment."

"You left yourselves wide open," Jeffrey said.

"No, we didn't. We came upon him, not the other way around."

"That's what I'm saying. We can't live in fear," Bunny said. "Even if we pretend we're not afraid."

"Well, poor people *are* scary," Teddy said.

"That's not what this is about," snapped Bunny.

Jeffrey looked at Teddy as if he didn't understand anything at all. The women crowded around us and Jeffrey stared at all of them, then started working on them. This is what he did best. They shared their own stories of fear. Walking the dog late at night near the water and hearing scurrying sounds or voices. Someone was trying to take away what we had, or benefit from it, at the very least. And this was unacceptable to them. The man hadn't attacked us. There was always an influx of people in the summer. Unknown variables, friends of friends, but they somehow seemed invited because they looked like they belonged. I walked these streets constantly and never felt unsafe before.

I looked to Teddy for help, but Jeffrey just sat there egging them on. He said he had always seen shadowy men wandering the streets at night. People he had never seen before. There was no telling what they would do if they thought they were under siege. They had a lot to fight for.

"Aren't your men going to protect you?" Jeffrey said to the ladies.

"How?" asked Teddy.

They all giggled nervously as Jeffrey leaned back in his seat. "If your husbands don't feel like protecting you, I will," he said.

They giggled even more.

"It's my gentlemanly duty." Jeffrey knew just what to say both to emasculate other men and be boastful. I waited for him to add something like "protect you from the Big Bad Wolf" or something cheesy like that. Porno bad. He didn't watch those movies in front of me, but I could hear him sometimes. I'd put my ear against the door and hear a furious tugging and slapping. I don't know why I listened. I was just glad he could still get it up. I wondered what he was thinking about, that's all. Didn't he know that we were both just masturbating in other rooms, far apart, wanting the same things, just unsure of how to get them from each other anymore?

I stared at these women and wanted to know where their husbands were. I scanned the bar and looked at the line of men in polo knits. It looked like their wives had dressed them—muted yellows, blues, a few stripes. The older ones were hunched over scotches, defeated by wrinkles. The younger ones, the ones that I had started to like, had

close-cropped haircuts, neat striped polos tucked into pressed khaki
golf pants, and no overhanging guts. They were still talkative and pos-
tured for one another. They talked about their orthopedic surgery pro-
cedures from the week or maybe the legal proceedings they had taken
part in. They looked like they still had some excitement about life left in
them. Perhaps they could still be appreciative. Whatever the case, their
wives were still slim and sitting next to them. I leaned in and put my
arm around Jeffrey and he looked at me, wondering what I needed from
him. I pulled my arm away as he scooted his chair forward.

"Oh, Jeffrey, Larry's got nothing on you."

I looked up, raised an eyebrow. Nora, sixty-five and thick-legged. What
was she doing with her short white hair and hip swivel? She was wearing
long shorts that hit above the knee and bright pink lipstick. I was worried
that she'd try to kiss him and leave a smear of pink on his cheek that I
would have to wipe off.

Her husband had left her and their twins the year before and now,
after the divorce was finalized, she was still trying or perhaps just begin-
ning to try to make her ex-husband, pale green polo at the bar, jeal-
ous. But he didn't even turn around. Someone said they had heard her
whispering "Do you want to fuck?" in the ear of a visiting sailor from
Rhode Island. After that I heard her crying to a friend at the pool about
the arrangements couples here made. Couples got bored, they needed
to have some spice, but everyone was okay with it and everyone was
supposed to go home when it was time to go home. Their arrangement
had been compromised and her husband had stopped coming home. I
looked around the room and wondered how many of these couples had
an accepted tolerance for indiscretions among friends. Revelations like
that had made me wonder why no one had ever asked me and Jeffrey
to join them in various entanglements. Or had they asked Jeffrey and
he'd declined? Or was I the only fool here without a willing extracur-
ricular partner and marriage workaround? I'd considered the stories

about boat trips to Block Island that ended up with mismatched cabin partners club folklore, never wanting to visualize, but maybe I was just being naive.

I had to laugh. At least someone like my mother was honest about who she was. These women, eyeing one another like every friend had the potential to leave strands of hair behind in their bed.

Bunny pulled Nora aside and the others clustered around, talking about safety.

"If anyone can get this problem under control, it's Lori," Leslie said.

They looked at me and nodded and I knew that no matter how involved I really was in the protection of our homes, I was a club member's wife for little more than a decade and I would always be the reason their friend was gone, no matter how unfounded that was. No matter how many husbands they slept with, I would always be worse. Jeffrey leaned back in his chair and smiled at them all, his white chest hair sprouting from the vee of his knit polo. I stared at him, acutely aware of his age. His hair was white like Nora's; maybe they were a better match.

They walked away and I said, "That man didn't do anything."

"If he peed on the street, that's doing something," said Jeffrey.

"He didn't really chase us, he just kind of stood there," I said.

"You're splitting hairs."

"Who cares?" Teddy asked. He looked at us both and mumbled something about needing to go to the bathroom. He got up and his chair toppled behind him. He leaned down to pick it up, but people were already staring, and it was excruciating. I stared down at the white tablecloth and noticed spots lining the lip of my plate. I tried to scrub them away with my nail. They would not budge and I could feel Jeffrey watching me. I wished Teddy would come back quickly.

"Don't you think everyone's just overreacting?" I asked.

"You're missing the point," he said.

"Illuminate it for me," I said.

"People worked their whole lives to live here. It's an investment of time and money that makes us owners. We own this," he said, waving his arm.

"You don't own the water, you don't own the beach."

"Yes, we do," Jeffrey said. "It's in our deeds."

"Who is 'we'?" I asked, because I knew he didn't mean me.

Even after all that trying, I never got to feel a real sense of ownership. I wanted him to say it out loud, to say *I don't mean you*, but he wouldn't. I was begging him to say it, so someone would finally be direct with me. So I would have a reason to feel like I never even had a chance. Instead, we stared at each other in a standoff.

I heard Teddy's laughter coming up the steps and I knew I would be off the hook now. We would have to talk about his failings now. Or sit in uncomfortable silence. Either way, I was no longer the bad one. I glanced up quickly to see if Jeffrey had noticed that Teddy was on his way back and he was looking around the room absently, watching the other club members laughing and talking. Teddy sat down and said, "I'm starving," and I saw that he had a new life to him, smiling. I saw the steaks coming our way, resting in the juice of their own blood. Teddy turned his head to see what I was looking at and saw the steak Jeffrey had ordered for him. Teddy looked at me, pained. I knew he didn't want it.

He cast his eyes down to the plate being set before him and watched the blood sluice from one side of the white plate to the other and he didn't even pick up his fork.

"I'm not complaining, but I didn't want this," Teddy said.

"You'll eat it," Jeffrey said. And Teddy did. He ate it all.

CHAPTER FOUR

TEDDY

MY STOMACH WAS CHURNING from all the red meat my father made me ingest. Or maybe it was because my buzz was fading. I searched through my pocket for something to make my buzz feel better and found an oblong white pill, which I figured had to be some kind of downer, and took it pronto. I was sitting on the deck of the club, watching the boats float in the marina and listening to the bells jangle each time a wave came in. This was what I liked. The sound of the boats made me want a life like this for myself. I could have a boat with some witty bullshit written across the hull. Nothing obnoxious like "Blo Me" like that idiot from school, as if somehow taking off the w made it less sleazy. I wanted classy. I'd fucking sail it into the sunset and end up on Block Island and squat there in the summers. I could be like one of those mysterious recluses who seem very desirable to women. I couldn't see our boat in the slip from here and decided that I would have to investigate.

If my father let me, I could have this life, and I would make it good. I wasn't weak. He just didn't know what I was capable of. No one did.

I had a leg up and that made it easier to slack off. I didn't have to work at the feverish pace that new guys worked when they came from nothing. I knew I was lucky. When my father used to take me to his office, I could pick them out. They worked like it meant something and never took vacations. They were trying to surpass their numbers. They picked up the proper sales keywords quickly: opportunity instead of problem, scalable sales implementation, and even that rah-rah shit about seizing your future and all the bullshit that led you to believe that anything was possible. They were always the brightest with the firmest handshake. The guys like me, who came from where I come from, had a little bit of a wrinkle in their shirts, and sometimes they decided Top-Siders counted as proper office attire. Those were my people.

I looked into the lit windows of the Captain's Lounge at all the guys a decade or more older than me and I knew most of them worked for this life. I already had an advantage, because I was a legacy. Did it feel good? I don't know. I sure didn't feel bad about it. The women stood in packs, away from their husbands, and none of them looked appealing to me. Well, that's not true. Some of them did—young-looking moms like the woman I'd just met in the bathroom. I had accidentally peed on the toilet seat and was cleaning it up when I heard a click-click-click and thought to myself, Some old lady, a lady who lunches, had wandered into the wrong bathroom, and I considered jumping out and scaring her, but then, you know, they're so hopped up on Chardonnay and Xanax, one false move could end it all.

So I finished wiping the seat, because cleanliness is key, and opened the door to the stall. And there she was. She wasn't old at all, just teetering a little bit. After she informed me that I was, in fact, in the ladies' room, she chased me into the hallway and made me shake her hand with my unwashed hand and told me her name was Jill.

I looked for her in the crowd of older, more successful versions of me but didn't see her. Leaning back, I stared out into the sky and heard the patio door open. Then there she was, my Jill, like she knew I was thinking about her. She was teetering more now, but not enough to make her look sloppy.

She swayed close to me and sat down. She said something like "Hey you," and I smiled back, happy that she remembered me.

But she didn't remember my name, so she leaned in close and asked me to introduce myself again.

"Teddy," I said.

"Like the bear?" She giggled.

No, that shit never gets old. I wish she knew that she didn't have to search for that thing that she thought would put me over the edge. I was just happy to have someone to talk to who didn't have some bull-shit preconceived idea about me. She could find out the truth from the other club mothers tomorrow.

She looked familiar, like I'd seen her around here before, maybe on my school breaks. But I didn't tell her that. I just nodded and smiled.

She laughed and told me that she was only teasing. She smiled extra-long while she said it, like she was trying to be sexy. I understood what she was trying to do and I tried not to be sad about it.

"Did I see you wearing a bat-wing thing earlier today?" I asked.

"You mean the Earlywine ladies' poncho? Yes, that was me."

"I don't even understand how you would put something like that on. Where do you put your arms?"

"You can put them anywhere. You can put them down your pants, up your shirt, no one would know."

"Damn," I said.

"I bought it."

"Good idea," I said.

I lay back and closed my eyes and she asked what was wrong. I told her that I didn't feel well and maybe I should go. She asked me if I wanted her to take my temperature and I wasn't sure how to answer anymore. The game was already old. I wondered if my mother had ever gone around bored and talking to strangers like this. If my dad allowed it or encouraged it. I thought about it for a second and then decided I never wanted to have that thought again. She wasn't around to defend herself, anyway.

"Is your husband in there somewhere?" I asked.

"How do you know I'm married?"

"Because they don't let single women in here," I said.

"They don't, huh?"

"Bad for morale," I said.

She smirked and said she guessed it would be. I considered her age and how many children she might have, or how long she had been try-ing. This was a family place, so people who weren't starting families, like me, made everyone uncomfortable.

"Why don't you tell me something about yourself?" I asked.

"Like what?"

"I don't know. A secret," I said.

She closed her eyes and slid down in the chair and giggled. "I don't know you well enough to tell you my secrets."

"That's the whole point. I don't know who you are, so I'll never tell."

She kept her eyes closed and said, "Maybe I had too much to drink."

I knew it was time for her husband to come find her. I wanted to go down to the dock, anyway. I slipped down the stairs. The bells on the boats jangled in the wind and some had their cabin lights on. If things got rough, I could live on the boat, I thought. I passed the big ones first, the Last One III and Ruthless for the guy who bought his boat after his divorce from Ruth, a real ballbuster of a woman who watched everyone out of her bedroom window.

And then my favorite, Dr. Luewken's boat—Sir Osis of the River. How did these old fuckers come up with these names?

I found my dad's small boat next to these monsters. Simply named

Joanne after my mom. I'm sure Cheryl loved to see that, Joanne in big sweeping cursive letters, when she climbed in. My dad had wanted to change the name, but I wouldn't let him. She had loved to sail, the water. When I was younger, I had convinced myself that some part of her was still down there. Shifts of light off the side of my boat told me she was. I used to take the Sunfish we had out and spend hours tooling around in the water, just talking to her like she was ever going to say anything back. My dad never dealt with the boat, just left it to drift around in the slip year in and year out. I was pissed at him for letting it fall into disrepair like this. It looked so small and weak next to these other shining boats, each a measure of its owners' girth.

Pauline had found out I was home and texted saying I could come over if I promised to fuck her; it seemed like as good a place as any to go. I knew that I could do better, because she treated me like I was something really amazing. We both knew I was doing her a favor and she let me do whatever I wanted to her, which was nice.

She was all right looking, but what she really had going for her was that she had an amazing assortment of painkillers. Her dad suffered from some kind of degenerative knee thing and he always got top-shelf stuff. It was easier to fuck on Percocets than drunk and it just seemed like more fun. Less labored and I could go for longer. If it were up to me, I'd always fuck on painkillers. She whispered "Teddy" in my ear when we fucked and it sounded accusatory. So I said, "What?" And she started pouting and said, "Nothing." And then I realized she was just trying to be sexy, but it wasn't working.

Pauline was sort of chubby around the waist and when she was lying down she looked flat and thin, but when she'd get on top her belly would hang over and hit my stomach as she bounced up and down. It was somewhat disconcerting. Equally fucking weird was her need to exercise on the elliptical machine in her parents' bedroom after we had sex. She always did it and her thighs rippled with every step. I closed my eyes and listened to her huffing on the machine as I was lying there, naked and surrounded by fake ivy plants. She shook me awake and told me I better get dressed, I couldn't stay over because her parents were coming back early in the morning. I felt like a child again and knew that I had to find a girl who had her own place.

Her parents' bathroom was repulsive, with clashing floral patterns on the wallpaper and shower curtain. Her father was obviously ball-less. I would never stand for this shit. I shook my head as I rifled through his medicine cabinet. Along with the usual Percocets and Vicodins I found some really great shit: Dilaudid. Mr. Kemble had turned into quite the pill popper. Thirty dollars each on the street last time I checked. I took five. No, I decided to take six. I thought about taking more. I probably wasn't going to see Pauline for a while and did I really even care if she got into trouble? Dilaudid was golden, not something you find in every-one's medicine cabinet. I wondered what was wrong with him. Maybe he was dying. Then I felt bad. If he was in that much pain, I probably shouldn't take all of it, so I put four back. It would give him enough time to get a refill. I wasn't an asshole.

I kissed Pauline on the way out and promised to call. I always did, but she always ended up calling first, never giving me a chance not to. Maybe this time she wouldn't call. I always thought that and never got lucky.

I went back to the Joanne to sleep in the cabin.

Tomorrow, when I woke up, things would be different, I thought to myself. I would get my life in check, maybe sail somewhere first to clear my head. I could go to the Cape or even farther up to Maine. I needed to know I could do things like this—be alone and self-sufficient. I had gone as far as Fishers Island at the mouth of the Long Island Sound in high school once. I was proud to have gotten there on my own and I wanted to keep sailing, go on forever, but for some reason I got scared. Like I couldn't do it, like it was a mistake to go in the first place. The open ocean looked choppy and I chickened out. I had spent the afternoon watching bigger boats with waving families sail past me into the Atlantic as I sat hunched over, drinking beers, wishing I had the guts to run away.

I woke up and didn't know what time it was, but it was so nice out that I decided I would go sailing and save the pills for later. No one was on the water yet, but I saw the sailing instructors readying the Sunfishes for the little kids. In the daylight, I could see the boat was in worse shape than I'd thought. From the looks of it, seagulls had spent months dropping oysters and clams onto the deck of the boat, scattering seashells everywhere. I picked them up and threw them overboard, uncovering the grime underneath. Why did my father even bother keeping it in a slip if he was just letting it waste away? I went back into the cabin, looking for cleaning supplies. *Poor Joanne*, I thought. I would bring her back from the dead. I spent the morning cleaning every part of the boat until she glistened. No one paid any attention to me as they wandered around the docks, and that was just fine with me. Men in deck shoes and white shorts showed off their boats to their friends, talked about the Cape, the Vineyard, and sailing down to Florida.

I pulled at the sail and started the engine, motoring out of the small harbor past the kids who had started crowding in around the Sunfish boats in their life preservers. I could hear them complaining as I floated by—it was too hot, their life preservers were itchy, one even pointed to me and said, "He's not wearing one!" I gave him the finger.

They all turned to look at me and I waved at the annoyed instructors as I passed. Once out in the sound, I cut the motor and opened the sail. It felt good to be out here alone, just listening to the water.

I was happy it wasn't that choppy and I hugged the edges of the islands trying to get a closer look at the houses. I took my shirt off and raced along the waves, trying to get to my favorite island. When I got there, I hung back and stared at the Tudor house and watched three little girls all dressed in white chase one another in circles. I would have thought they were ghosts if I hadn't seen their nanny, sitting up by the house with a book, not paying any attention to them. I sailed around the island, stared at the tennis courts, at this world cut off from the mainland and seemingly cut off from time. I sailed out farther, away from the small cruise ship calling out state history and the power boats with guys drinking beer and looking for rocks to jump off of. I didn't recognize any of the guys yelling off the side of their boat, but I knew the Coast Guard would probably roll up on them soon enough. I held the rudder tight and sailed away from all of them. I ran my hand through the water and thought if this was all I ever had to do I would never complain.

CHAPTER FIVE

CHERYL

WHEN I WOKE UP in the middle of the night, I noticed that Jeffrey was not next to me. His side of the bed was clean and made. As I snuck down the stairs, I could see him asleep on the sofa, a pillow crammed under his head. I got the familiar feeling in the pit of my stomach of having done something wrong. I had put on a lace nightgown last night just in case, but it hadn't mattered. Jeffrey hadn't seen me. I could walk around like a nudist and it wouldn't even register with him. Now, when I returned home from my morning walk, the sofa was empty and I folded the blanket that he had tossed aside. There was no point in being melodramatic.

The club phone directory lay open on the counter. I stood above it and ran my fingers along the numbers. I flipped the pages, closed my eyes, and pointed.

Tuck. I wasn't going to call him. He'd recognize my voice, tell someone. I closed my eyes and chose again. I didn't recognize the name and I dialed *67 to block my number, then I took extra care dialing, listening to the beep with each numeral. I listened to the phone ring and when a man picked up, I said a breathy hello, waited for a return of the favor, and got nothing. He hung up. That was the problem. Often I was mistaken for a telemarketer or someone begging to change political parties. I wasn't. I just wanted to get us off.

I tried to phone my mother. It rang and rang, with no answer, not even a voice mail or a machine picking up. I considered driving over to see her, just to see if she was okay. I decided I would do it after another walk. I needed to clear my head and think of how I would approach her. I knew she wouldn't be happy to see me. The last time I had seen her I'd told her I was ashamed of her. I used to watch my mother float through the house at night in her lace see-through nightgown, unashamed as we watched her. She was the most beautiful woman in the world to us. We wanted to be womanly like she was. I wanted to be looked at and desired. As I had been gangly and young, it had seemed to me an impossibility. I'd had to wait years to fill out.

She was always pacing and waiting for our father, but she looked so gentle floating back and forth, her nightgown billowing behind her with each step. Her heels would tap against the wood floor and hypnotize us with the sound. When she wasn't home, we'd take her heels out of the closet and try to mimic that sound as we paced and puffed on invisible cigarettes, looking out the window for our father, trying to capture that same exasperation. When our father stopped coming home, she took to waiting for other people's fathers, but we didn't wait with her then.

There were times when the men would bring us food and we'd be fed for a while. But sometimes she would be gone for days and we'd have to search the house for spare change or for some of the rolled-up money we saw them give her when they thought we weren't watching. We'd take it, knowing she would always get more, then run to the store and stock up on TV dinners, breakfast setups with smiling parents on the packages, frozen treats we wouldn't save for dessert. When she was home, she'd prepare a feast of whatever she had. She made it feel elaborate and special. Once, she had come home with a watermelon, exclaiming it was too hot to eat anything else. She cupped a melon baller and dipped it in and out of the flesh of the watermelon, making a hillside of sticky red balls on a plate. She cut out stars to put on top of the overflowing plate. She said we could eat it all; it would fill us up. Then she gave us each a cube with a dusting of salt and told us to pretend it was the main course, the rest could be dessert. Juice flowing down our chins, we ate until our stomachs rumbled, sick from the sweetness. She said some people never got to taste watermelon even once in their lives and we got to eat one whole.

My mother always dyed her hair a brassy blond and when she wasn't entertaining, she put it up in curlers with a thin, gauzy scarf wrapped around it. But when she unwrapped the curlers and pulled her fingers through the loose waves, she looked beautiful. Her face never betrayed her sadness about being abandoned or about our sister Laurel, who had died before she even turned two. Her slender calves and shapely hips filled in her dresses just so as she wandered the house night after night. As I got older, I would put on the laciest of her bras and imagine taking them off for someone. I kept my hair long and blond, not as bright as hers was, though. I had her body everywhere and displayed it casually, like it would always be perky for me. I was happy that I had studied her femininity well enough to capture it. But I was no longer making use of it. The subtle, daily humiliations had finally taken their toll on me because nothing I tried worked any longer.

When our father left, our old rotary phone would ring and my sisters and I would fight like rabid dogs over who would answer it, hoping it was him, but it never was. My sisters spent less and less time at home, wanting to be away from all the sadness, the outline of missing people too grim. Boys would take them away, my mother would yell, warning them they'd end up like her, alone with a brood of ungrateful girls of their own, but they didn't listen. Neither did I.

I remember the thrill of hearing my first feverish call—a man breathing into the phone, asking for Roberta. We would hang up on them and run away, or sometimes, if the phone would ring and ring, we'd leave it off the hook. Our mother would chase us around then, calling us brats and worse. But the phone kept ringing and I started picking it up and I wouldn't hang up when I heard the begging voices. Instead, I'd let my voice go gravelly and low and I would ask them what they wanted exactly, then I would try to give it to them. Sometimes they wanted me to laugh in their ear, sometimes they wanted me to tell them what my dreams were, sometimes they just wanted to know what I'd do if we were alone in a room together. I would wrap and unwrap the phone cord around my index finger and watch it go red, the blood just under the skin wanting to burst out. Sometimes, my mother would follow the cord and I could feel the tug as she picked it up and walked with it down the hall and into the pantry, where I was hiding and whispering about my see-through panties. She'd yell at me, but I would run, and eventually, they only called for me. I had to leave then, as our resentments became unbearable and the house became a tomb to everything we had lost.

I opened all the windows, the smell of reeking fish drifting in. Jeffrey hated when I opened the windows. He had the thermostat turned to 64 degrees and expected the temperature to stay that way. Why live on the ocean when you could never smell it or feel it? The gardeners were already working, trying again to re-seed lawns that had stubbornly refused to grow after being flooded with salt water during last summer's hurricane. I stared out at my own garden and saw weeds poking up from around the fence. I opened the doors, went outside, got down on my knees, and started pulling. The rocks were already dotted with fishermen and I wondered when they'd be pulled off for ruining someone's view. I saw the old man and his dog weaving their way back along the rocks and waved, but he didn't see me.

I went inside and laced my binoculars around my neck and decided to take off for the nature trail. It was quiet as I walked through the tall reeds and onto the path and bridge. I wanted to see if the man under the bridge was back. I made a point to check. I looked down, saw no legs, no body at all, and was disappointed. I pulled out my binoculars and scanned the reeds. I was having bad luck today. The fledgling chicks had still not arrived. I was reaching down to clear some pebbles out of my shoes when I heard whistling behind me and froze.

I turned to look and didn't see anyone there. The whistling stopped. I briefly panicked, thinking the fisherman I had called the police about had followed me.

On the bridge, I was surrounded by marshes and beach, the water and islands in front of me. I saw the sailboats floating out, white and tall in the water. On the other side of the bridge were thick trees and underbrush. The whistling started up again, and I hoped someone would come through biking. A woman with a stroller, anything. It wasn't a bird call and it wasn't the wind. It was a distinct whistle. It was him. I knew it was. It had to be. He was following me. I was disgusted that Jeffrey and Bunny were right. I didn't want to be called out as the fool, have them pity me because I was naive and still believed people were capable of good. I breathed in and out slowly. Maybe it wasn't the fisherman, maybe it was a bird lover like me. I was just overreacting because I was alone.

I put my bird book back in my pocket. I could go farther down the trail, over the second trolley bridge, or head back through the marsh. Why would someone be hiding in the marshes and whistling? It didn't make any sense. Calm down, Cheryl. *Calm down.* There were more nests down the trail and I didn't want to go back home yet. I wasn't ready to face the drive to my mother's house. I was starting to lose my nerve.

As I walked into the wooded area, the whistling stopped. *Thought so. Some stupid kids, that was all.* I kept walking. Ahead was a small, rusted-out bridge covered in graffiti. Teenagers always wrote the dirtiest things. Like everyone wanted to know who they wanted to fuck or love. What did they really know about either? Branches cracked around me and I stopped, but I didn't want to turn around. Wind rustled the leaves around me and the nature path seemed very empty all of a sudden. Where was everyone anyway? It was a beautiful day, high tide, birds everywhere. Where were the kayakers at least? I heard the rumble of a speedboat in the distance, but otherwise, just the wind and the crackling of underbrush.

I was scared.

I convinced myself that I didn't have to look, that no one was behind me. I just had to walk a bit faster.

I felt the weight of my binoculars. They could harm someone. I gripped them tightly and kept moving toward the trolley bridge. There were more pebbles in my shoes, jabbing me through my thin socks. I decided to just keep moving.

I was hearing things. The stress of Teddy coming back, Jeffrey being upset. The situation with Lori had me rattled. That's all it was.

I checked my pocket and realized I had left my phone at home. *Of course, Cheryl.* It didn't even matter. Everything was going to be okay. I would be home soon, and in the future, I would ask friends to come on walks with me. Even Bunny!

I could see the clearing and the trolley bridge in the distance and I knew I would be okay. At the other end of the bridge, in town, there was open water and boats and people. A ball field. Maybe I would walk the streets home. It would take longer, but there were cars passing often.

The whistling started again. It was a tune I didn't recognize and if I turned around it would be to accept that there was indeed someone behind me.

I wasn't going to do it.

I could feel myself getting hot, sweating. Tinges of panic that I was trying to keep at bay. I started to power walk.

What was that tune? It sounded so familiar. I had heard it before.

On the ground I saw a rock, something that could fit in my hand, and I reached down to pick it up and then kept walking. If it was someone I knew, someone from the club playing a trick, and they saw me wielding a rock on the nature trail. . . Well, let's just say I'd be a laughingstock.

If it was the fisherman, then everyone would tell me how right they had been all along and I would have to nod and admit that their hatred was not misguided. I would have to do that even if I was wounded; I would have to tell them they had been right all along.

I slowed my pace so the would-be attacker could catch up with me. I wanted him to think that he could get me and that he was winning. The whistling was getting closer and I couldn't take it anymore, so finally I turned and threw the rock as hard as I could.

I saw it flying through the air and then it hit the man squarely in the face. He fell, crumpled, to the ground.

I covered my mouth with my hands. It was Steven. I had smashed him above the eye.

I screamed. "Oh God! I'm sorry!"

I looked around. How could no one be here? How could there be no one to help? I ran toward him and he was lying on his back, his face covered in blood and moaning.

"What did I do?" I said.

I looked at Fran Cronin's teenage son, Steven. Lori's bad house sitter Steven. Nice legs Steven.

What was he doing following me? I looked him up and down and inhaled sharply. I recognized his sneakers.

His penis was hanging out of his pants. He was going to do something to me. Or maybe he was just peeing. Maybe this was a mistake.

Then Steven sat up and reached for me angrily, saying, "I know you." Grabbing my arms hard, he said, "You want it."

I looked down at his still-erect penis and black pubic hair blossoming out of the slit in his boxer shorts and zipper hole. I struggled away from him and in a panic I picked the rock back up and hit his face again. I heard the crunch of tooth and bone. His mouth was a bloody wound as I dropped the rock.

I backed away from him. He was lying in the middle of the nature trail, bloody-faced, with his penis hanging out. He wasn't even circumcised. I kept backing away and he called out, "Help!"

I backed away and started to run. I wanted to get away from his moans and the plovers who were running now, too, back to their nests. I didn't stop until I reached the inside of my house. I slammed the door behind me and leaned against it, breathing hard.

My feet ached from the pebbles and I pulled off my shoes, starbursts of blood coming through my socks from the small wounds.

I clutched my neck. My binoculars were gone. Jeffrey had had them initialed for me. I felt dizzy thinking that I had left them beside the body. No. He wasn't a body. He was still alive when I left him.

"Hello?" I called out.

My voice cracked when I said it. Was I supposed to call the police? He had wanted to hurt me on the nature trail. I had to do what I did. I stared down at my hands. There were specks of blood on them. Steven's blood was on my fingers. I went to wash them, limping.

"Hello!" I screamed again.

Where were my binoculars?

Jesus Christ.

There was hardly any blood. Maybe a little splatter. Splatter. What was I thinking? I scrubbed my hands furiously.

In the kitchen, my face was hot and I felt achy. I tore through the cabinets. Where was the bleach? I looked down and saw that there was a tiny bit of blood on my tank top and I ripped it off.

His penis was out, Cheryl. It was OUT. This was not your fault. It was his. And he counted as a full-grown man. He wasn't some boy. He just had a young-boy face. He said that I wanted it.

I poured the bleach over my hands and my nostrils burned. I went back to the bathroom and dumped the rest of it down the sink, in case there was any blood there. I stared at myself in the mirror. *He grabbed you, Cheryl. He wanted to hurt you. You are not a bad person.* You were defending yourself. You didn't want it. He was using the nature trail as his private jerk-off spot and that was unacceptable.

I had only seen him socially a few times, once possibly at a Christmas party. Had he been one of the carolers that had gone house to house last year? Yes, he had a sweet voice, the only one in the group who could carry a tune. He knew I took walks. And yesterday I had said he probably had nice legs to Lori. She would remember that. She would tell people I was asking for it and he was just a child. She was that kind of gossip. My hands were burning. Would there be fingerprints on the rock? I had no idea. Maybe I should have called the police. What if he told on me? Would I go to jail for leaving the scene of a crime? I gripped the sides of the sink and tried to hold myself steady. I found the hydrogen peroxide and poured it over my feet, listening to the sizzle and pop. I cleared out bits of dirt and sediment that had crusted onto my toes with the peroxide swell.

I went over and picked up the phone. My hands stunk with bleach. I started to dial 911, then hung up. I had to ask Jeffrey what to do. I dialed his office. No answer. Then his cell. No answer. I tried again. It went to voice mail after two rings.

I put the phone down. Unsteady again.

Jeffrey should have been at work still. And Steven could have been discovered by someone on the trail by now. I didn't hear any sirens, though.

So I just sat down and waited, careful not to touch the couch with my hands in case there was still bleach on them. I looked down and realized I had no shirt on. I threw my tank top in the garbage and covered it in leftovers from the fridge: mixing spaghetti and sauce with whatever blood might be on it. I couldn't even begin to imagine where Teddy was. I ran to lock all of the doors.

CHAPTER SIX

TEDDY

"PAULINE, GET OFF my dick."

She always laughed when I said it. It was too easy. She rolled away from me and back onto her lounger and we sat in the sun, drying off. Kids had taken over the pool, and old ladies swam laps in lanes. There was nowhere for us to go. When I came back from sailing, I saw Pauline putting her towel down on a pool lounger and thought, *Why not?*

"I wish I was on your dick," she whispered.

"Jesus." I groaned and put on my sunglasses, waiting for her to stop talking. She turned over, looking pissed. Whatever, there were finally hot women at the pool, even if they had kids with them. These moms weren't wearing those bathing suits with skirts anymore. One woman even had a bikini. It was Jill from last night. She didn't have a butch haircut like everyone else, but she had a rock like the rest of them that I couldn't really compete with. She looked at me; I saw it. Pauline's eyes were shut tight, so I took off my sunglasses and checked out Jill in her bikini.

She caught me staring and took a long time pulling herself down the pool stairs and because she was right in front of me, I knew she was doing it for me. She inched down and made the necessary "it's so cold" face. I was close enough to see the goose bumps on her arms. Her arm hair was blond, not like Pauline's coarse black hairs. I had taken a risk being seen with Pauline in public. My moment of weakness was giving people the wrong impression. They would think I didn't care about aesthetics. You are, after all, only as good as the people you align yourself with. Her presence could be viewed as toxic to my success, especially with lonely women. I should have been studying sales training manuals instead of being by the pool, so I had to make this count.

Luckily, Jill finally dipped back in, careful not to get her hair wet, and she swam after her kids, who were trying to splash her. I could tell she was letting me watch her. She made a big show of it and I looked at the other mothers, the ones with the short-short haircuts and one-pieces and tight white shorts cutting off their circulation, and I knew they were watching her, too. She was new here and she wouldn't last long if she kept acting out some kind of pool fantasy, my pool fantasy, splashing around and squealing like that.

"God, shut up," Pauline said.

I guess she wasn't impressed, either. She covered her face with a magazine. *Cosmopolitan.* "How to Orgasm 6 Ways." Bullshit.

I returned my attention to Jill and she gave me a little wave. *Fuck, I can't do this*, I thought. She had kids. She didn't have any good secrets.

I looked up and saw old Elaine put her arms above her head and shake out. She had skin like jerky that cascaded down in flaps around her bikini as she tanned by the pool day after day. Cheryl usually tanned with her, but I didn't see her today. Where was she? Busy making my dad a meal? Cleaning her visor? She had been all right when she first started coming around. I could see what he had seen in her. She had been young and pretty hot and hadn't had the drunken bloat my mother had. I don't think anyone in the world had. Cheryl had been so happy and grateful for the opportunity to be his wife, to be let into our community.

Jill got out quickly and made an even bigger scene of drying herself off. I liked watching her, I wasn't going to lie. She had a nice hard body and she knew it.

"Stop looking at her already," Pauline said.

I got up and started putting on my clothes.

"I was kidding. Where are you going?" she asked.

"Home."

"Let's go to mine," she said.

I told her I didn't feel like it and she started to pout. Jill brushed past me, and even though we didn't touch I could feel her.

I think Pauline knew it, too. She screwed up her face and asked me what I was going to do at home.

"I gotta talk to my pops about some opportunities," I said.

"Fuck him and fuck opportunities," Pauline said.

She had her fine points, but respect for her elders wasn't one of them.

"Come on, Pauline. This is serious," I told her. She looked back at me, annoyed. It was hard sometimes when you were the only one who was trying to give a shit.

Old Elaine was staring at us both, waiting for something to happen. She always took her top off when she lay down on her stomach. Who was ever going to see her tan lines, anyway? Pauline tugged at my arm and I looked down at her.

"Are we going to go or what?" she asked. I told her I was going home and slid my feet into my flip-flops and walked away. I could hear her getting pissy and packing up her stuff, but I couldn't deal with it, so I kept walking.

As I rounded the corner up toward our street I saw cop cars at the Cronins' house and I wondered if Steven had gotten busted again.

That guy was always pushing the wrong people. Bigmouthed people. Fucking idiot. I remember the morning they found tire tracks all over the third hole at the golf course when we were in high school. At first everyone thought it was an accident, and then they realized that someone had damaged the course on purpose. After that, there were always headlights beaming out from the golf course, waiting for it to happen again—someone was always on guard, wanting the assholes to come back. They behaved like they were always under some kind of threat.

It didn't end there. Each time they put up big white signs welcoming people to LITTLE NECK COVE, A CONNECTICUT BEACH ENCLAVE, they were set on fire or spray-painted. The new homes that were being built on Spruce were vandalized. Everyone thought it was townies, people angry that everyone in Little Neck Cove wanted to separate and have their taxes flow back into their own community for flower street dividers and not into the public schools in town. But it wasn't them. It was us: me, Joe, Steven, Chucky, and Rob. That's what was so funny. It was us all along—their own children doing it to them.

Steven was a fucking sicko, though. When we were kids, he would take french fries from the snack bar and slide toothpicks into them, then wait for the seagulls to swallow the fries up. They'd fly away, up into the air, and the toothpicks would pierce their throats and he'd watch them fall out of the sky, one by one. Or he'd catch the gulls and tie their legs together, clipping their wings and leaving them in the road to be run over. He was always weirded out by the fact that we weren't into torture as much as he was. We all had to draw the line somewhere.

There was a crowd forming near the cop cars, mostly old ladies on their way home from women's doubles. A couple of golf carts stopped in front of the house, clubs still attached. I wanted to know what was going on, but I also didn't want to be implicated in anything. I sold him the rest of my leftover bad shit the other night and I didn't want to get my face in anyone's memory. I was done with selling, anyway.

At the house, Cheryl was sitting on the sofa looking so out of it. She eyed me suspiciously and I thought she might have heard the sirens or something.

"Are there police outside?" she asked. I told her they were swarming and she ran to the window to look.

"They're not coming for you, Cheryl. You can open the curtains. Jesus."

She was not fucking amused.

"I'm not hiding," she said.

"What's wrong with you?" I asked.

"Where are they?"

"There're like five cars in front of the Cronins' house."

She looked at me like she really wanted to tell me something. All she said, though, was: "Steven, oh."

I wanted to say, *Spit it out, Cheryl. Why are you so fucking weird?*

"Are you going out?" she asked.

I told her I had just been out. I was tired and going upstairs. She literally stuck her hand out and I raised my eyebrows like "What?" until she had to let me go.

"Stick around," she said. "At least until your father gets home."

"I said I was tired," I snapped at her.

CHAPTER SEVEN

CHERYL

I DIDN'T WANT TEDDY to leave me alone, but I didn't know how to ask him to stay. I called my mother three more times while I waited for him to come downstairs, but she never answered. I wanted to tell someone what I had done. If she'd had a machine I would have confessed to it. I would have said, "I hurt someone terribly." But no machine picked up, so I kept my mouth shut. I stared out at the ocean and saw that the sun was moving lower in the sky. Where was Jeffrey? I tried his phone again. This time it went straight to voice mail. He was somewhere that he shouldn't be while I was "leaving myself open."

There was a commotion outside and I ran to see what was happening. I peered out through my front window and saw police cruisers. I felt like vomiting. They knew, Steven had told them. I was going to tell the police about him, about what he was going to do, and they'd realize I was the victim here. People were coming out of their houses to see. Where was Jeffrey? Everyone would see, everyone would know. Things would be said about me and I wasn't even sure that Jeffrey would defend me. If Steven had thought I wanted it, would other people think that, too?

I opened the door, tired of waiting. I would go to them and simply explain that I had been too scared to call the police.

"I didn't do anything!" a man yelled.

I was startled when I saw two police officers push a man down on the ground and straddle him, fishing poles flying.

I backed away, like the rest of them. No one knew why the police were apprehending him, but I had an idea. He was not in this much trouble for illegal fishing. I knew then that I was a terrible person because I wouldn't come forward. This man was saving me from everything and I was letting him.

"What's going on?"

Teddy was standing behind me, wrapped in a towel, wet hair dripping on the rug.

"You should get dressed," I said.

"What are they doing to that guy?" he asked.

"I don't know," I lied.

"Maybe it's because of whatever was going on at Steven's," Teddy said.

I shook my head, thinking about what a bad job Steven's mother had done of bringing him up. That boy used to do terrible things. Now, nearly an adult, his evil had accelerated. His mother was always protecting him—*Not my son, he would never.* I did the world a favor.

"Is he dead?" I asked, nearly hopeful thinking about it.

"What?" Teddy asked.

He eyed the man on the ground. "No, he's still moving," he said.

"Not him," I heard myself saying.

Teddy looked at me like he knew something about what I was talking about.

"What's all this now?" Jeffrey said, striding up to the house. He looked perturbed, inconvenienced.

Teddy and I stood side by side and glared at him.

"I had to park in the club parking lot. I couldn't even get into my own driveway," he said.

"Where were you?" I asked.

He set his briefcase down and went to see what was going on, ignoring me. The policemen were still straddling the fisherman on the ground. When were they going to let him up? I noticed a teenage girl standing and looking at the man on the ground. They could have been related. Jeffrey noticed her, too. He was eyeing her in a strange way. She was saying something in Spanish that I couldn't understand and she wouldn't stop crying. He started to go over to her and then thought better of it and turned his attention back to the man on the ground, but not before locking eyes with her.

Everyone was watching the display and Jeffrey walked up to the policemen like they weren't even busy.

"What do you think he'll do?" I asked.

"Probably tell them they're creating an eyesore," Teddy answered.

We stared as the man tried to wriggle free and then at the cop who was trying to calm down Jeffrey, who was pointing and acting animated. We were too far away to hear what he was saying and I considered stepping closer, but I didn't want the policemen to get a good look at me. My guilt was overwhelming, but I could not move. I would not help that poor man. Jeffrey came back in a huff.

"What did they say?" I asked.

"There's been an attack," Jeffrey said.

I covered my mouth and realized my hands still stunk of bleach. I quickly shoved them in my pockets and decided to re-check them for blood when I was alone.

"Who was attacked?" Jeffrey looked back at the police and I quickly glanced at Teddy, who was looking at me.

"We don't even know the whole story," Jeffrey said.

"Let's not jump to conclusions then," I said.

"Do you want to identify him?"

"What?" I asked.

"The man from yesterday. Is it him?" Jeffrey pointed to the man on the ground. His arms were being zip-tied.

"No, of course not," I said.

"You didn't even look," Teddy said.

"Will you both leave me alone? I hardly saw him," I said.

"Damn, Cheryl. Chill—"

I could hardly hear the last part because I was rushing into the bathroom.

"Are you okay?" Jeffrey asked.

"Fine. Fine." I got my bearings straight and walked out of the bathroom. My nostrils were still burning from the bleach, but there was no more blood anywhere on me.

"You've been really off lately," Jeffrey said, like an accusation.

"Something terrible happened today," I started.

"I wish that you could possibly understand what kind of day I had. I can't listen to your outrage about vagrants right now," he said.

Right then, I realized I couldn't tell him anything. He was not going to be compassionate. He was the you-left-yourself-open kind of blamer.

"I hope you remember we're going to Elaine's house tonight," he said.

"I think I have to call her and tell her I don't feel well," I said.

"It was your idea and she's your friend. It's too late to cancel."

"Where were you all day, anyway? I called you more than once," I said.

He looked at me as he walked up the stairs and didn't say a word, like he didn't need to answer to me. I overheard him telling Teddy that he had gotten him a spot in Richard Shepard's office. He would have to interview, but it was just a formality. Teddy said something like he wasn't sure he wanted to work there and Jeffrey got loud.

I went to the window and saw the police cars driving off. The fisherman was gone and the area where they had thrown him down was just dirt and stray gravel from the Magrees' house.

"Do I have to go, too?" Teddy asked behind me, his voice like a small child's.

I stared out the window and mouthed a low "No."

Jeffrey still wouldn't answer my question about where he had been all afternoon as we walked to Elaine's. I was carrying a Tupperware container of cookies that I had found in the pantry. Keebler or whatever. Jeffrey wouldn't let me take the Danish ones. He said they were his favorite. I would hide the cookies behind everyone else's food and if anyone asked I would deny I had brought them.

"Something terrible happened," I said once more.

"I'm sure we'll hear all about it at Elaine's."

"Was a woman attacked?" I pressed.

"They said a teenager was attacked. A kid."

A kid! A kid! Steven was no kid. I felt ashamed for being excited about his lingering look. He was a predator. An uncircumcised predator. Jeffrey looked at me as I worked to catch up with him.

"Why are you limping?" he asked.

"I hurt my foot earlier."

He asked me where and I almost said the nature trail. I caught myself just in time. Instead, I said, "On the rocks, by our house. I'll be fine tomorrow."

"Look," Jeffrey said.

I looked. Steven was standing hunched over with his mother farther up the street. His face was bandaged. *I did that,* I thought.

"Who knows if he just got in a fight with someone and doesn't want to tell the truth?" I said.

"We should go talk to them. See what happened."

"Don't revel in someone else's misery," I said.

"You know that's not what I'm doing."

I felt Steven watching us. I could hear him saying "You want it" over and over again.

"Maybe he was asking for it," I said.

"He's a victim, Cheryl." Jeffrey tugged at my arm and leaned in, breathing hot on my neck. "Get it together," he said.

I looked up and Steven had disappeared with Fran into their house. I still felt his presence, though. And him watching me. I looked into all the windows of the houses we passed as we walked the rest of the way to Elaine's house.

The living room was filled with people and they were already drinking cocktails. Elaine was wandering through the room in a caftan with a big turquoise flower in her hair, and I thought, *Oh no, it was going to be one of those parties.* The ones where she hoped everyone would drink too much and stay too late and it would be like old times. Key-party times in the early 1980s when everyone was still youthful and supple-skinned. When their children were young and could be tucked away quietly. When cocaine flowed freely. Later, when their marriages started fraying, they all started trying to behave, or tried to keep better secrets. I looked at them, some in their midsixties now, and tried to imagine just how wild they had been. I thought about the things that had happened in this room and how it was haunted with other people's regrets. When I reached out for Jeffrey, he was already gone, working the room. I went up to the built-in bar, from when Harold was still alive, and the bottles were all still intact, the top ones dusty and with faded labels. I scanned the wall and wondered if alcohol got old, then grabbed for a bottle of vodka, slightly warm. I ignored the laughter around me and concentrated on slicing a lime wedge, and when someone brushed up against me, I pretended not to be alarmed, but I was. Everything was making me feel nervous and I hoped I didn't still smell like bleach.

Rob Girardi was smiling like we hadn't just seen each other the day before on the greens, like he hadn't yelled at me from his cart to get moving because I was holding up the men.

"Where's your better half?" he asked.

I waved toward the crowd of people. All couples—the Picards (always hoping), Mary Ann and her husband, Larry. Christine was there, too, with her doctor husband keeping her in check. Tuck was nimbly peeling away the skin of the figs on the paper plate in front of him, trying to make eye contact so that he could start a conversation with someone. His wife sat next to him, laughing and full of light. She was luminous with her silken blond hair and straight white teeth that positively glowed against her tan, freckled skin. Everyone looked at her happiness and wanted to absorb it. She must have been pregnant again. They were all sitting in pairs. Except for Debbie Picard, who was sitting on the arm of the three-seater sofa, too close to Larry.

"Somewhere in there," I said, and Rob laughed.

"Heard he squared off with the town police today," he said.

"The fishermen," I added quietly.

"It's bigger than those people," he said.

He leaned in close. "Didn't you hear?" he whispered, like he really wanted to warn me.

"No," I whispered back. "What?"

"There was an attack."

He nodded his head and clicked his tongue against the roof of his mouth. "Attempted murder, they're calling it."

"That's absurd. I saw him walking. Just now," I said.

"He was really messed up, wasn't he?" Rob said, still clucking. "Irreversible damage."

I almost said, It was probably just a few broken teeth, a cut above his eye. *I could have done worse.* But I kept my mouth shut.

Rob put his hand on my shoulder to steady me, to show his support. "The family is beside themselves. Our whole community, naturally."

He said things like "our community," "how could this happen," "used to be safe," and "what was happening," but all I could do was scan the room and look for Jeffrey. Rob made me sound like a monster, not someone trying to defend herself.

"It's so terrible. It's an unsafe world for everyone," I said. "Did he say who did it?"

Rob didn't say anything for a long while. He just looked at me and I felt flush again, dizzy, like I had said the wrong thing, the thing that was going to get me in trouble and get me caught, because I said it before I asked if little Steven was okay. Rob gripped my shoulder like he wanted to feel my pain and soothe it and then he told me that they had a suspect but weren't sure, were still looking, and were sure it was someone from somewhere else.

He had hairy knuckles and he rubbed my shoulder with his hand. He told me it was probably a pervert who did it. He leaned in close and said, "The kid was half undressed."

When he leaned in, I could smell the scotch on his breath. He told me the family didn't want that part getting out, but that he knew he could "trust me."

He looked me in the eyes long and hard until I pulled my face away from his. I felt a slap on my back and it was Elaine in her caftan, laughing.

"I'm going to have to pull the plug on you two soon," she said, a little too forcefully. She thought she had a claim to all the men who were only tenuously linked with their wives.

Her lips were rimmed with a frosty lilac lipstick. She bought it at the Walgreen's in bulk. It was called Amethyst Smoke. I knew because I always saw her pulling it out at the pool when we were tanning and she needed to reapply it. For moisture, she said. She had tubes of it loose everywhere.

"We're just talking," I said.

She snorted. "Almost had his mouth on yours," she said.

Rob rolled his eyes and said, "I've got one at home." He walked away, letting his hand stay on my shoulder for as long as he could, stretching his arm out long. No one wanted to deal with a drunk Elaine.

"Watch that one; he's about to be in the middle of a nasty divorce," Elaine said.

"Who isn't?" I said.

"Not many right now, actually. Everyone's trying to keep their shit together," she said. "The economy is bringing back cohabitation."

"I'm glad it's for all the right reasons," I said.

"There's love, too. Of course."

I stared down at my glass and Elaine asked what I was drinking.

"Vodka with a lime wedge," I said.

"You'll be drunk in minutes."

I swirled the lime in the middle of the glass. Maybe that was just what I needed. Elaine took it away from me and hurried to the bar and dripped in pomegranate juice, the new cranberry.

"Have some, it's good for you," she said, handing it to me.

I gulped it down and looked for somewhere to sit.

"You don't have to drink it like a shooter," she said. And then she told me I looked pale.

"I'm fine. Just tired."

"A lot of shit happening around here," she said. "It's like Juarez all of a sudden."

"Like you've been," I said, suddenly feeling bold.

"Of course not. They kill you there, Cheryl. Kidnap you and kill you just for being American. Didn't you see those water-skiers on *Dateline?*"

"I didn't see that one."

"It was chilling," she said. "Hacked to death."

"You're so dark," I said.

"That's life. Look at poor Steven. Now that's *dark*."

Everyone started talking about Steven then. Fran Cronin's boy, poor Fran Cronin's boy. Plastic surgery was going to be needed. He was undressed. They lingered on that fact, as if he was the victim. He was turning into some kind of misunderstood hometown hero. I looked around the room at the men, and at the newly reappeared Jeffrey, now sitting near Debbie Picard, who laughed and laughed, nearly in his lap. He looked positively bored with her and I was glad.

I looked at all the men and stared at them as they leaned back in the sofa cushions, smiling and saying, *undressed*, as if Fran Cronin's son had suffered some kind of rite of passage. And I saw all of them with their pants down, holding their penises out and stroking them.

I grabbed on to Elaine's arm and clutched it so violently that she yelped.

"You're hurting me," she said.

"Do you see them?" I asked. "Do you see what they're doing?"

The men were all looking at me, the women, too. And Jeffrey looked at me the worst of all, embarrassed.

"This drink is too strong," I said.

I sat down on her wicker chair and nestled my drink in between my fingers, cooling my hands down long enough to be able to run them along my forehead, trying to calm myself down. The couples were still sitting around, talking and laughing. Ignoring me now. No one had their penis out; there was no energetic sound of stroking.

"Honey, maybe you should go upstairs and lie down," Elaine said.

I went up the stairs, clutching the railing, and into her room, then checked the window to see if anyone was on the street. It was summer-evening desolate.

I lay down on her bed, a beachy room with a knitted blanket and sheets and shams with a Ralph Lauren hydrangea print. I tugged at the blanket. It looked as if Elaine knitted it herself, but I knew that she hadn't. She had probably gotten it from Knitters Korner in town. Probably for around five hundred dollars, which was a shame because it was clearly a synthetic yarn.

I leaned back on the pillows and hoped that nothing lurid had happened on them, You could never know with Elaine. She was very vocal about never wanting to sleep alone.

Someone stepped into the bathroom and I heard a strong stream of urine. The walls were so thin. I rolled over, trying to cover each ear. It had to be a man. Bad prostate or something. I heard the toilet flush and footsteps and prayed they weren't headed to the bedroom.

"You okay?"

I turned over, unsure of whose voice it was. Tuck was standing there, smiling and looking around the room.

"Too much going on down there," I said.

Downstairs, when I'd had my vision, his penis had been small and squat. I stared at his crotch, unable to look away. I didn't see a bulge, so I thought I had been right on the money. Here was me wanting it, everywhere.

"I conceived my first kid in this room," he said.

I glanced at his face and he wasn't looking at me at all; he was staring at the walls, remembering and smiling. I tried to stay silent and not intrude on his memory.

"That was one hell of a party. Elaine's parties have gotten tamer over the years, if you hadn't noticed." He said it in such a melancholy way that I wanted to hug him suddenly, wish that night back for him.

"The room didn't look like this then," he said. "And I didn't look like this." He looked down at himself, at his creased shorts and faded green polo shirt. He chuckled and patted his small belly.

"You still look fine," I said.

"You think so?" He was so alert just then, so searching.

He pulled out Elaine's vanity stool and it was much too small for him. He looked like he was about to share something with me and I wasn't really sure I was up for it. I leaned my head against the pillows and closed my eyes.

"I like you better than Jeffrey's first wife," he said.

"I have been worried all night that you didn't," I said, half smiling.

"Well, come on now. I'm sure you hear the opposite all the time," he said.

"Only as I'm leaving the room," I said.

"She was a very unhappy woman," he said.

"Wouldn't you be?" I asked.

"I really can't blame her. But if you tell anyone I said that I'll deny I ever talked to you." He paused, then said, "Jeffrey's a tough nut to crack."

"Try being married to him," I said.

He was staring out the window at the Magrees' house, their over-built second floor, thinking about something.

"Gilded cages, right?" he asked.

"Maybe."

"Let loose. Say what you feel. Talk shit."

"I'm doing what I'm supposed to do here," I said.

"Hmm. I guess, I'm sure whoever you are is pretty good, too."

I narrowed my eyes at him and he looked at me, lying on the hydrangea sheets, tight hair bun jabbing the back of my head, and I felt like he could see right through me.

"Uptight is the word I'm looking for, I guess," he said.

"We're all playing at something, aren't we?" I said.

"No, I'm just sitting here," he said.

"You're the one regaling me with your conception stories."

"That's what I mean. Don't you have any of those? Don't you have any indiscretions? I know you do."

"I don't have any kids," I said. And then I thought of Teddy, briefly, and for a moment was concerned about where he was. "I have Teddy."

"I mean sex stories," he said.

"Everyone has sex," I said. "Why is that a story anymore?"

He contemplated it for a moment. "I suppose you're right," he said.

"You're looking for first experiences behind a 7-Eleven in the summer? That kind of thing?" I asked.

"I mean, if you want to get that gritty, sure."

"I don't think you could handle it," I said.

I didn't have sex in exotic locations, just bed-and-breakfasts and places with sheets like Elaine's — an overabundance of floral patterns. If Tuck wanted to hear about how Jeffrey and I came to be, it would just be stories about dark parking lots and fumbling in his car. We liked it quick so I could get back to my post at the dressing room. When Jeffrey got more attached, it felt nice, and when he would tell me about his wife, I would listen and hold his hand and tell him he was a very patient man. I loved him because he loved me and we had so much fun on bona fide dates, going to museums and jazz festivals. He even took me all the way to Massachusetts once to visit Tanglewood and eat brie and listen to classical music in a big, rolling field. I realized that the appeal might have just been that I was from somewhere else and I wasn't after anything from him except his time. I didn't think these were the types of sex stories that Tuck wanted to hear.

He leaned back on the vanity and played with Elaine's things. Sniffed her perfumes, opened her jars. He looked at himself in the mirror and at me beyond him on the bed. He spritzed one of the atomizers and sniffed the air.

"I think I'll keep asking you the same question every day."

"What's the matter with me?" I asked.

"Bingo."

"Maybe you can just tell me. You seem to know it all," I said.

"Where's the fun in that?" he asked.

I stared at the ragged collar on his knit polo. I didn't think he had a right to ask, but he was the first person who had, so I considered my answer. His Top-Siders looked like they had a thin film of mold on them and were misshapen. I would never have let him out of the house like that.

"I never thought I'd live by the water like this," I said.

He stared out the window at the Long Island Sound spread out around us. I could hear high tide hitting the seawall that kept the ocean away from the houses.

"We're the lucky ones," he said.

I suddenly wanted to tell him all about Steven and the rock and what I had done. I thought he, if anyone, would understand. Now, sitting here with him, it didn't seem so risky.

"Do you think you're happy?" I asked.

Tuck nodded as he weighed the pros and cons in his head. "I don't really ever think about it," he answered.

"What do you mean?"

"I mean, I'm here. This place is great. I've lived here my whole life and I don't have to do much. Why ask the question? You're setting yourself up for trouble right there," he said.

I put my head back on Elaine's pillows.

"Probably true," I muttered.

CHAPTER EIGHT

TEDDY

WITH CHERYL AND MY FATHER gone I wasn't sure what to do with the rest of the night. My father told me I was supposed to show up at Richard Shepard's office in the morning to discuss my future as a surgical sales rep or whatever Richard did. The whole idea was giving me waves of panic. I needed to take something for my nerves. I also needed to put a lock on my door or something, because maybe Cheryl had figured out what I was doing. I was pretty sure she'd thrown away the clothes I left in the bathroom last night. They weren't in the hamper and they weren't in the dryer. I knew she was territorial and anal about cleanliness. Also, she was a snoop. If she threw my pills away, I'd be out hundreds of dollars and I'd have to go crying to my father, so that wasn't going to work at all. I found some in my jacket pocket—blue and round—and popped two in my mouth and held on.

I took a seat on the couch and turned on the television and ran my feet over the cold glass of the coffee table because it felt nice. I knocked over the club directory and when I picked it up I suddenly wanted to know just where Jill lived.

I didn't know her last name, so going family by family through the directory was a bitch. Finally, I found her in the Fs. Thank God. Jill Fulton. Husband, Craig. Children: Kimmie and Jennie. Both names ending with "ie" like it was a thing.

They lived on Graves Point and I considered driving by. I hunted around in my pockets and didn't feel my keys. I got up and my legs felt thick. I found the keys on the kitchen table and flicked through them, trying to find the right one for the car. Graves Point was only a couple of streets over and the kids were probably inside by now, so it would only be minimal damage if I hit anything. But was I really going to pull a drive-by like a girl? Was I?

I did it. Her house was mediocre, one of those old, ugly houses from the seventies. I assumed it was their starter home or something. I figured Craig would have been doing better for himself than this. At least get her one of those new Cape Cod numbers. I could do better than this. I would kill it as a surgical sales rep and then quickly move on to surgical sales manager and Richard Shepard would give me my own territory and I would be able to buy a house that overlooked one of the holes on the golf course. Maybe not one of the good holes, but one of them, anyway. That shit would be my starter home. Are you hearing yourself, Teddy? Do you hear your aspirations right now? They are so fucking attainable right now.

The windows were dark and I turned my car off. It was about six o'clock or something, so they must have been out to dinner or at Elaine's with everyone else. I could wait, because I had nothing else to do.

Their garage was open and the cars were gone. I wanted to see what Craig had going on in there. Nothing much, it turned out, except that he was an anal-retentive asshole. Even the oil cans were spotless. A lot of pool toys, shit like that. Nothing that told me anything about what was really going on inside of him. His fears.

I went around to the backyard and saw the most amazing jungle gym. It had like ten parts to it. All different colors. It was like one of the ones from an elementary school. What was with this guy? He built it? Nah, he probably hired some guys to do it for him but made sure his family was out so they didn't see what little he did to make it happen. He just handed over his AMEX and let other men do it for him. Manlier men. The slides had domes that you could look out of and there were like four of them. And monkey bars! I went over and grabbed onto the monkey bars and just hung there. There were fireflies blinking all around me and suddenly everything felt fine. I hung there until my arms hurt, just swinging back and forth.

Headlights filled the backyard and I knew Jill was back. I had tucked myself into the bubble slide and fallen asleep. She couldn't see me hiding in there, but I could see her and her daughters walking to the back door. With a pizza box in her hand, Jill looked like a mom. I decided to stay in the bubble slide and wait for them to go inside. For a second, she looked my way and I knew she couldn't see me, but maybe she just knew I was there.

The lights turned on in her house and I saw her walk into the kitchen. I wasn't watching her in a creepy way; I just wanted to see her doing normal things. Mom things. She turned away from the window and looked like she was saying something to one of the girls. I wished I could hear through the window, but I wasn't going to risk moving closer. She was probably one of those hands-on mothers, tending to cuts and bruises. Reading to them before bed. Could I blame my current state on my mother because she had never read to me? I wasn't sure.

Instead, I pushed myself up into the slide. It smelled like new plastic. Like her husband and his workers had just put it together the week before. I moved up until I couldn't see the grass below anymore. I pushed my head up until I reached the clear bubble in the slide and then I saw Jill open the door, and for a moment, I panicked.

She let a dog out, a golden retriever, of course. I bet its name was Max.

I wanted something about her to be new and surprising, something I hadn't thought of before.

Her dog came sniffing near the slide. It was so big, like a McDonald's PlayPlace or whatever it was called, that he had no chance of finding me. I just hoped he wouldn't start barking and fuck up my hiding spot. He pissed at the base of the slide. Nice.

And then he circled the slide and the jungle gym and I tried to move farther up, away from the bubble and out of sight. My hand slipped and I started sliding down, my feet slamming against the sides, making noise as I tried to stop myself. And that bastard dog started to bark. Jill came back outside.

"Bogey."

Jesus Christ, that had to be her husband's choice for a dog's name.

"Bogey. Come here."

The dog didn't listen to her. He just kept barking at where I was trying to move up, trying to be quiet. He snarled, baring his teeth in my direction.

"Bogey! Is it a raccoon?" He was going crazy.

She slammed her foot down on the patio and called his name again. He ran to her and I was impressed. He actually listened to her. More important, he wasn't going to rip my balls out of my pants.

She stared at the jungle gym for a while, the dog pacing behind her, and finally went inside with the dog, shutting off the kitchen lights.

I waited in the slide for a while, contemplated sleeping in there, but it was getting sort of warm and my shirt was soaked through with sweat, from the stress of it all.

Lights turned on upstairs and I knew it was safe to leave. I went down the slide and made sure not to step in the wet spot of dog piss, then slowly walked across the backyard. I looked up at Jill's window, where I thought she'd be, and she wasn't. And for a minute, I was disappointed.

CHAPTER NINE

CHERYL

I STOOD IN THE front yard, snipping my Mr. Lincoln roses and trying to figure out what was causing the white spots on their leaves. They had developed a sickness and no amount of mild dish soap or garden-center nutrients was helping. I held the patches of oval leaves in my hands and inspected them closely. Were the leaves being eaten through to the veins? The buds looked haggard but were still trying to bloom despite the attack. I swabbed each leaf with a Q-tip dipped in a solution I had made myself. Vinegar and some other homeopathic remedies. The swabbing would take all afternoon or longer, but I needed to save them. I had to give them a chance to survive.

"What are you operating on?"

I looked up and saw Tuck on his bicycle.

"I'm trying to rescue my roses from whatever disease is eating them alive."

"Do you suspect foul play?" he asked. "The pisser?"

"I think we're calling him the urinator now. Anyway, he was peeing on the street, not in people's yards."

"Urinator. That definitely sounds more threatening than pisser."

"It really does the job riling up people at association meetings," I said.

I stared up at Tuck and held my Q-tip with purpose and said, "Anyway, who would want to hurt my roses?"

Tuck looked up and down the street, then said, "Maybe someone has a problem with you. I heard Lori talk about the tree. Don't you know how people around here operate? You don't cooperate. . . they send a message."

"There's more evil ways to take me down than to mess with my flowers," I said. I looked at Lori's yard. Everything was blooming beautifully.

I shook my head.

"She just wants to watch you crack slowly, that's all." Tuck smiled at me when he said it. Like he knew it was happening and he wanted to lighten the mood.

"I'm sorry about your flowers," he said.

"You know when you finally find a sense of purpose? Like, something needs you in order to grow and thrive, you take it seriously. Roses are temperamental. What else do I have?"

"Probably nothing, like everyone else around here. Though there's purpose and then there's purpose," Tuck said, smirking. "Do you think I want to spend my weekend mowing and weeding like the rest of these suckers around here? Mulching, spreading little colored rocks around just so? Lori imports her own sand, did you know that? Did you know that? She didn't like the color of the sand on her part of the beach. Twenty thousand dollars for sand."

He stared at me, waiting for my disgust. "Twenty thousand dollars for a different shade of sand. Why aren't you outraged?"

"Obviously, because I didn't know. Who does that?" I asked.

"Exactly. Who does that? It's all just going to wash away one day.

Then what?" he said.

"It could, you're right. Storms have been worse and worse each year," I said.

"Watch Florida be wiped off the map this summer. Then we'll be stuck with them year round."

I stared up at the blue sky and said, "I have to make sure our flood insurance is up to date."

"Just let things be. Don't need to control it all, you know what I mean? Just let the world spin and we'll all be okay," Tuck said.

"Did you ever follow the Grateful Dead?" I asked.

"Only in high school, why?"

"You remind me of every Deadhead I ever knew," I said.

"I could see you on the arm of a Deadhead."

"I even followed them one summer," I said.

"No shit?"

"Yeah, one glorious unshowered summer with my boyfriend. What a disaster."

"Did you have dreadlocks?" he asked.

"No, but he did," I said, laughing and embarrassed.

Tuck told me all the good ones had. I looked at his thinning hair and thought of Charlie and wondered where he was now. He probably looked like some middle-aged dad somewhere—collared shirts and loafers. Finding former boyfriends online always made me feel so old. I wondered if I looked their age or if I had willed myself to stay young. I had noticed frown lines forming in inopportune places. Continual sadness and lack of sleep did terrible things to a person's face. I had stopped my dawn walks, taking them later in the day for safety. Tired and sunburned, I'd restlessly pace and ache in the humid air.

Mary Ann rolled up in her golf cart and said, "We're having an emergency association meeting to discuss violence and trespassing. Are you two coming?"

"Why are you making it in the middle of the day when most people can't come?" Tuck asked.

"It's an emergency," Mary Ann countered. "You can ride with me." She pointed at me.

I hopped in her cart and Tuck trailed behind, wobbling his front wheel.

"Are we having a vote?" I asked.

"What's going on is a travesty," she said.

She wheeled toward the association building slowly enough so that I could see the new, more insistent signs that were popping up around the neighborhood. Now our dogs weren't allowed on the beach, either, walks had to be conducted in designated areas, and people watched from their windows to make sure you picked up the piles of shit left behind. I hadn't even seen who put them up. As we pulled up to the building, I saw other carts lined up in a row. This was serious.

I heard the battle cries coming from inside the squat building and couldn't do it.

"Mary Ann, I really have to go home. I left the tea kettle on. I'll be right back."

She eyed me suspiciously, like I wasn't committed to public safety.

"If you don't come back, you can't vote," she said.

"Of course I will. This affects all of us," I said, turning. I didn't see Tuck. He had purposely lost us. I could not face a room full of retirees arguing about immigration lockdowns. I left Mary Ann and walked by the Cronin house, close enough to be able to see through their windows. No one was home. I couldn't imagine him keeping quiet for this long. I knew the police had been by the house. What had they told them? And if they asked for a sketch, I couldn't imagine what he'd conjure up. I thought about confronting him, but I had no idea how that would turn out. He was unpredictable.

CHAPTER TEN

TEDDY

I HAD SPENT MY MORNING filling out forms and going through the motions of an "interview" with Richard Shepard. He told me about Brainshark and Salesforce training. Everything sounded tactical. Like we were waging a war with our products, like the opposition couldn't win against our implementations. Now it was after lunch and I was given a cubicle of my own. The walls didn't reach higher than my chest so I could see what was going on in the adjacent cubes. Exactly nothing. The woman next to me had pinned all kinds of photos from vacations with her boyfriend or husband on the walls of her cubicle. Each photo was the same except for a different theme-park backdrop—legs outstretched, hands in lap, holding on to each other like there was no greater love anywhere. Beside the photos were certificates of excellence with her name loud and proud: STACEY CHURCH. STACEY CHURCH. STACEY CHURCH. The guy on the other side of me had crystal awards with his name inscribed on each one. His superior salesmanship on view. He was working it on the phone, closing the sale. He had words of wisdom printed out in huge letters pinned to the walls of his cubicle: IS THIS THE BEST USE OF OUR TIME AND/OR MONEY? WILL WHAT I'M DOING HELP RESHAPE ARIBACORP'S FUTURE? I considered what my motivational printout would be. Of course: ASS GRASS OR CASH: NOBODY RIDES FOR FREE. Looking around, I knew that shit would not fly here. None of these bastards looked like they had a sense of humor. They were in it to win it.

My cube neighbor slammed the phone down and tapped his fingers on his desk. Logged his sale without looking up. He had just made money while I was standing there like a jerkoff mocking him. I saw him scribble "$10K" on his legal pad with four exclamation points after it and do a silent fist pump under his desk. He looked around to make sure no one was watching and saw me staring at his fucking winning self. How do you ask a guy like that how he does it? You can't.

"Nice job," I said and sat down in my ergonomic office chair. *I should have gotten high for this*, I thought.

"Oh, your hair!"

People were streaming in from lunch and I didn't want to turn around but I did. A woman stood messing with her hair at the edge of one of the cubicles. Other women surrounded her and I figured they weren't much older than me.

"I gave it all to Locks of Love," she said, waiting for the onslaught of praise. It came. Everyone around her looked at her like she had done something truly wonderful. She said, "My hair feels more age appropriate now. And that's a good thing, right?" She played with her bangs and then said, "Well, maybe that's not a good thing."

They all told her that it was a great thing she'd done. I rolled my chair closer to my desk and hunched over my computer keyboard. I felt them looking at me, but no one said anything. Instead, they started talking to the guy next to me. They traveled in packs, each pack walking over from cubicle to cubicle to chat. I didn't think I'd make it here. I knew I wouldn't. I stared at the woman with the haircut while someone else said "Heather" and waved her away like she was being ridiculous. They all lied to her in different ways to make her feel better.

I wondered what her hair looked like before. She motioned her hand at the middle of her back and said, "Remember when my hair was to here yesterday? Do you all remember?"

They nodded in unison and she repeated the words "Locks of Love" several times while she waited for everyone to tell her how good a person she was again. And they did. She told everyone she had baked a special cake for the occasion. Rum raisin. She laughed and said they would be drunk from her cake before the quarterly meeting. They all laughed with her and looked at me as if I didn't belong there. They offered one another pieces of it, every cubicle except mine. They all ate the cake and Heather asked them over and over again if it was good. If they were enjoying it. If it was delicious. She told them about each ingredient. She told them about the things she included that weren't in the recipe. The risks she took. She wanted to hear that they had paid off. I looked at her and thought, *What the fuck does she know about grateful cancer patients?*

I left the office early and took whatever pills I could find in the car. I drove in circles and watched the boats and killed time before I was supposed to go home. I needed to act like I had worked a full and productive day. There was a crowd outside of Milligan's as I drove by, so I pulled in real quick. Inside, the restaurant's wooden benches were filled with families eating clam strips and tourists eating the overpriced lobster dinners.

At the bar, a few people recognized me from town and did the back pat. A few screamed out my nickname and pounded the bar. The bartender looked at me with a fucking annoyed expression on his face and I instantly regretted coming in.

I ordered a Guinness and sat at the end of the bar, scanning, looking for anyone good. It probably would have been a better bet to cruise over to Don Julio's, where there was a chance tourist girlfriends were drinking bowl-size margaritas while their tourist boyfriends watched cable TV in the adjacent motel rooms. I could bring one of them back into my car and I'd never have to see her again, she'd be halfway to Cape Cod by the next morning.

I hoped Pauline wouldn't show tonight, get grabby and put her owner-ship trip on me. I didn't want to risk it. I finished my beer, choking it down while I made my way through the restaurant and to the back patio. It was loud and some radio station was being piped in through the speakers—Creedence, Aerosmith. I knew it was a more townie crowd out here. The patio ended at the edge of the marshes and every-one was crammed together pretending it didn't smell like rotting fish or lobster remnants. Huge black garbage cans were strategically placed near the railing for beer cups and corncob husks. I walked toward the bar, a makeshift banner with a line of plastic yellow flags announcing CORONA SUMMERS waving above the bartenders.

I ordered a Bud and stood around awkwardly, wishing I'd taken a little bit of a hit before I got out of the car. It was warm and the air was humid, but it felt all right out here. A few families were picking through lobster carcasses but otherwise the tables were emptying because of the early-evening mosquitoes. What the hell was I going to do? What would I tell my father, that the "day in and day out" at that place would fucking kill me? That I didn't want to be a part of any rat race? I knew what he would say. *Suck it up.*

"Teddy?"

It was an unfamiliar voice and I was afraid to turn around.

When I finally did, I didn't recognize the girl, but she was small, with a nice chest and runner's legs in supremely short shorts. She looked ner-vous and that made me nervous. Was she from some previous summer?

"Yeah," I said.

"Tracy," she said awkwardly.

Still no fucking clue.

I smiled and nodded like she was jogging my memory. I would have remembered those legs, probably. At least the tits. Anyway, she looked too young for me, for sure.

"We hung out on Block Island," she wavered.

I knew what she meant by "hung out," but I still couldn't place her.

I kept nodding like a fucking idiot and smiling wide. I heard myself telling her how good she looked and how it was great to see her.

And then she asked for her wallet back and I knew exactly who she was.

Block Island. Sand. The guys. The reeds. We were wasted. We did it anyway. She passed out and I took her wallet.

I felt fucking sick all of a sudden and leaned over into one of those big trash cans and threw up.

She just stared at me, her hand out. I don't even remember where I put the wallet. It had been our summer of collecting trophies. Maybe I lodged it into the couch of the summer house we were partying in. It didn't matter. It was gone now and she was staring at me and waiting. She didn't give a shit that I just threw up in front of her and the families still outside, trying to enjoy their meals. I was a fucking terrible person.

The song faded and the DJ screamed, "THESE ARE THE SOUNDS OF SUMMER YOU'VE BEEN WAITING FOR. LOW RIIIIIDER."

The music started up again and I felt helpless as waves of nausea hit me and I started to sweat. There was an acrid smell coming off me, like a sickness. I just smiled and nodded my head in agreement to nothing in particular and started moving toward the door, and away from the waving plastic yellow flags advertising endless summer fun.

CHAPTER ELEVEN

CHERYL

WE SAW A COMMOTION up ahead as we pulled our golf bags behind us through the club parking lot.

"What now?" Jeffrey sighed.

I could see neighbors pointing and yelling at someone and a dog standing by, confused. As we walked closer, I knew it was the old fisherman and his dog. I picked up my pace and saw Lori yelling at the old man.

"Hey, leave him alone," I said to Lori and Mary Ann, who was flanking her. "What's he done?"

Lori looked at me, enraged. "We put up signs. He's not supposed to be here."

The old man held his bucket full of fish and looked at me. Jeffrey stood next to me, silent.

"He's not hurting anyone," I said.

"It's okay," the old man said.

"Lori, let him be," Jeffrey said as he tugged my arm, trying to pull me away.

"We can't bend the rules whenever we feel like it. There are ordinances, least of which is no dogs on the beach."

"Cut the shit, I see yours there all the time," Jeffrey shouted.

The man put his hands up and said, "It's okay."

Lori and the others turned their attention back to the old man. Lori pointed at his run-down truck and said, "We're sorry. This is private property."

They weren't sorry, but the man nodded and said, "It's been beautiful here for a long while. Thanks for the fish."

He whistled to his dog to follow him and dropped his bucket in the bed of the truck, opening the door for the dog. He pulled out of the parking lot with a plume of exhaust as our neighbors watched, electric with their newfound power. I looked at Mary Ann, with her shoulders back and chest out in boast, and saw a flicker of shame on her face as she averted her eyes from me. Her shoulders curled down as she fixated on a pile of stray court clay. *You are spineless*, I wanted to shout as they turned and walked back to their houses.

"You're taking this too far," Jeffrey called out.

"This is about safety," Mary Ann shouted, not bothering to look back.

Jeffrey shook his head and stared at our disappearing neighbors. We sat down on the curb, silent for a long time.

"What's happening here?" he asked. "How'd it get to this?"

We sat there until the street lights came on and moths crowded the light.

"Cheryl, I'm unhappy," Jeffrey said.

I had the sense that he had spent weeks drumming up the courage to say this to me right at this moment.

"I know you are, too. I don't know why you have to keep pretending like everything is fine," he continued.

"I don't think everything's fine. Do you want me to cry so you can see how not fine I think everything is?" I asked.

"I don't know what happened, but nothing's working anymore," he said.

"I know this isn't working, but it can," I said.

"I just feel worse and worse about us. I can't give you what you need."

"How do you even know what I need?" I asked.

"It can't be this," he said, looking at me as if he was embarrassed that I had put up with the way things were for as long as I had.

I felt like I needed to stop this from happening somehow. I heard myself saying, "I can try harder." Even though I didn't think I would.

I even went as far as saying, "I can be better. We can get it back to how it used to be, you just have to want it." Jeffrey looked straight ahead and nodded, like for a second he wanted to believe it, too.

Then he said, "I don't think so."

We got up and squared off. I didn't know the right thing to say to make *him* wake up and be better. Where would I even go? Back to my mother? I had given him everything. Why was he the only one who got to choose the outcome? The lines on the asphalt were crumbling and cars were slowly driving by, weaving by us the minute their headlights picked up our lonely outlines.

"Is it someone else? Is that the problem?" I asked.

"It's just you," he said. "It just went away."

"Get it back. Bring it back. You can't just run away every time."

"Do you think this is easy for me? Do you think I want to feel this way?" he yelled.

I didn't know why he wanted me to feel sorry for him, for his position in this, but I did for a moment.

"You're not thinking clearly. You need some sleep," he said. "You can't possibly want to stay in something so toxic."

"Don't tell me what I should think or want. I gave you everything."

"That's not a reason for anyone to stay," he said, as if it were a fact.

The yelp of seagulls filled the air and I watched as a car came tearing onto the road, its headlights heading straight for us. I walked toward them.

"Goddamn it, get out of the road!" Jeffrey yelped. Then he jumped out of the way without reaching to pull me to safety. And the car swerved to miss me and drove through the metal fence of the tennis courts and straight over the clay, finally stopping at the net and rolling over. Jeffrey was standing against the curb as we looked at each other and then at the car, recognizing it as Teddy's.

"What's wrong with you?" Jeffrey asked me.

We ran toward the car together. The headlights were still on and illuminated the deep grooves in the clay, the hard silt spread everywhere, the lines pulled up by the pegs. We saw that the driver-side window was open and Jeffrey dropped to his knees. The mesh of the metal fence was imprinted deep in the clay and hurt my knees as I dropped down, too.

"Teddy," Jeffrey bleated.

He reached his arms into the car and tried to make sense of the darkness. Smoke and clay dust was sifting through the air around us as the car stayed on.

He said "Teddy" again and again.

Finally, we heard a sound and I exhaled for the first time.

The association security guard rolled down Club Parkway toward us. The track lights on the top of his Dodge Neon glowed orange and he pulled into a parking space and then stepped out of his car with no sense of urgency.

"Everything okay?" he asked.

"Call an ambulance!" I shouted.

He pulled his phone from his belt clip as he trotted back to his car. Jeffrey kept reaching his hands into the car, trying to tug. I reached for Jeffrey's arms.

"Jeffrey, you might hurt him," I said.

"Don't touch me," Jeffrey said, and I pulled back.

We both leaned down and tried to peer into the car at Teddy. He looked like a trapped animal. We told him not to move. He had a cut over his eye and blood poured out over everything, turning the scene gruesome. I held onto his hand while Jeffrey got up and ran to the security guard, whose name, I think, was Pete.

"Teddy, can you hear me?" I asked.

He was young again in that car seat, the first time his face betrayed his feelings in a long time. He wasn't pretending to be bad or good or adult. He was in there, mewling, scared.

"They're coming to help. They'll be here soon."

"Did I hit anyone?" Teddy whimpered.

"No," I said, hunched down low.

"I'm sorry," he said.

"It was an accident," I said.

"It wasn't your fault," Jeffrey said, coming back behind me to comfort Teddy.

I clutched Teddy's hand, my knees bruising on the ripped-up fence. I looked to see where Jeffrey was, but he had disappeared. I heard sirens and I knew Teddy heard them, too. I told him it would be okay soon, that they would get him out. I asked him what hurt as I rubbed his hand and he said, "I can't feel you touching me."

The club said the summer tennis tournaments might have to be scrapped because the courts were a disaster after the accident. Jeffrey had stayed silent about what we had talked about before the crash and I could only assume it was because he couldn't possibly handle taking care of Teddy alone.

The impact had detached two nerves in Teddy's right arm and rendered it numb and immobile below the elbow for the foreseeable future.

He sat in bed or on the sofa staring out into the ocean each day, just silent. Simple things like putting on a shirt or pants were suddenly difficult. He would snap at any suggestions of help because he was making an attempt at going it alone. I told him things like *you need us, we're here for you*, and other words of encouragement, but he only really said anything when we were going to and from physical therapy or the other specialists we had to see. And then it was just various words of disappointment and questions of *when* and *how long*.

I was still staying away from the nature preserve. No one asked me why. I knew Teddy wasn't happy, no matter what we did. I thought if I was kinder to him he would never suspect that I had walked in front of the car. He had never asked how we had gotten to him so quickly. Time always seemed distorted during moments of tragedy.

The only thing was, sometimes the phone would ring and I would pick it up and there would just be the faintest breath inhaling and exhaling on the other end of the line. Sometimes I would ask, "Who is it?" But the breath just kept rasping. Sometimes I would stay on the line for five minutes and just count the breaths. The person never hung up; I always had to.

The last time it happened, I whispered "Steven?" and waited for an answer. There was none. I started to think about the way he had looked at me when I'd seen him with Lori. His lingering glance had morphed into a sustained look and I could remember the color of his eyes. I picked up the phone again and dialed. My mother's number had been disconnected.

I had sent my mother another check and it was returned, too. This time I got it before Jeffrey did. I knew I had to go to her, find her. I was afraid of what would be there, but I had avoided it long enough. I didn't want to sit in the house with Teddy as he scratched his arm, hoping to get it to move, to have feeling again. He was leaving sores in the hard-to-see places, but when I helped him out of his shirt I could see his frantic attempts to prove that this was all temporary. I had to get out, even if just for a while.

Maybe my mother had moved to New Mexico to live with my sisters in some vast desert town. I looked up their addresses on Google Maps and stared at the space and destitution of their squat square homes. I tried to look up their numbers, but they were unlisted. I knew my attempts were feeble. I couldn't practice what I would say to any of them if I saw them again. *I chose him, I was wrong.* No amends seemed enough. I stared at the old trucks in their driveways and daydreamed about what their lives must be like. I saw cacti bent over in the sun in their front yards. I tried to move the camera on their streets and into their dirt driveways, closer to the windows so I could look inside, but I could only shift left and right along the main road. A hedge hid Vanessa's house from me. I wish I could see a person. I typed in my mother's address and clicked the street view on the map. A blue ranch with chipping paint. It seemed like autumn in the picture because the leaves on the trees were orange and yellow. I wondered how often they updated these photos. Had it been taken last fall? The fall before? Was her house really in this much disrepair? I tried to zoom in again and noticed a shiny material in the windows. I leaned closer to the computer screen.

My mother had tinfoil masking her windows.

I clicked the window closed in embarrassment.

I asked Jeffrey to take Teddy to his doctor's appointment and got into the car.

I-95 had fewer cars on it than usual and I thought about how Jeffrey hadn't even asked where I was going. He didn't care.

When we were kids, my sisters and I thought our mother's house was the world. The pond, the woods, and the farmland, where we would creep around to watch the cows sleep. We would hunt frogs and kick over stink cabbage, screaming as it erupted in the sulfuric smells of decay. Our hair would hang down loose around our faces as we used sticks as knives and pretended to spear each other, hunted for one another in the deep woods. We were always playing attack. Sometimes we'd crowd around the small stone headstone we had found in those woods. Laurel, it said. There was no last name. It was one of those hand-carved markers and we had different ideas about where it had come from. We imagined our mother asking one of her men to haul it out back for her, doing things her own way, not letting anyone know her business, not even us. We would run through the woods carrying our sticks high, chanting Laurel, Laurel, Laurel, resting only to cast spells of protection for our lost sister.

I parked across the street from my mother's house and looked up and down the road: modest homes dotted yards that were encircled by trees. The area was surrounded by farms or old remnants of farms. I hesitated before crossing the street, not wanting to move past what I had been able to see in the Google street view. The trees were lush and thick and bore down on the small blue house. The windows did indeed have tinfoil on them, crinkled in some places, and I shuddered. My mother would never . . . Our family home would never look like this.

I didn't know the woman who shut the world out with scraps of tinfoil and tape.

I finally made my way onto the lawn. There was no car in the driveway and I couldn't imagine she had ever cleaned out the garage. I couldn't look into the windows because of the tinfoil, so I went around the back, checking behind me to make sure no one was looking. All the windows had tinfoil on them, even the pane on the back door. What was my mother doing in there? I couldn't even begin to imagine. There was nothing in the backyard and it looked overgrown. The front yard did, too, as I walked back around to the front door.

I knocked and pressed my ear against it. I didn't hear a sound. She had taken away our keys when we left, saying she didn't like drop-in visits. It hadn't even crossed my mind. I walked into the woods and tried to remember the way we used to go to find our sister Laurel.

It was as if the terrain had changed completely. Missing trees and layers of dry leaves, years of them, covered up any sign of our little stone. I stood in the woods and thought about how fearless we had been and how fearful I was now, even before Steven. As kids, we had spent hours getting lost and never felt concerned about finding our way again. We were explorers, through and through. Sometimes we'd daydream about staying in the woods forever, being close to Laurel and building a family of wild girls. And now she was a nowhere girl, forgotten under all these leaves. I stared at our house through the trees and at the small window that used to be ours, the small gravel patch underneath it, and walked toward it.

On hot nights my sisters and I would strip down to our underwear and run around the room we shared, arms flapping like we were crazy. We'd lounge around reading fashion magazines and trying on our mother's makeup. We were in a rush to be women, to be looked at and admired. In the winter, with the wood stove burning hot in our room, we'd be nearly naked, window wide open, hoping the smoke would pour out, mouths up against the window screen breathing in the sharp, cold air. Sometimes we'd hear footsteps on the gravel and stare at the window, wondering who was watching us in the dark. We'd dare one another to take off our bra tops and we'd strut around in front of the window, trying to get the phantoms to want us, practicing at being grown up. We'd always aim ourselves toward the window when we'd hear that gravel crackle and put on a show. When we'd walk outside the window in the daytime we'd find crushed-up cigarette butts and our stomachs would tingle, knowing it wasn't a raccoon out there, or a possum, making all that noise. It was a man. Someone who wanted to look at us for a change, someone who couldn't get enough. In the winter we'd find them, too, covered in snow, wet through. We felt invincible then because we had all the power in the world. We were wanted, lusted after.

I walked up to the window now and kicked around looking for any cigarette butts, but the gravel was clean of them, and our small window was tinfoiled over, shutting it all out. I looked around and found a rock. I took it in my palm and hit the windowpane as hard as I could, then watched the glass fall inside the room. I stuck my hand through the broken pane, trying to unlock the window.

I felt the pain flash quick and pulled my hand out. "Damn it."

I saw the blood seep to the surface and flow out the length of my palm. I had gotten myself good. Running back to the car, I cradled my bleeding hand, trying to apply pressure on the cut. I found a cardigan and wrapped the sleeve around my hand, trying not to get any blood on the seats. The street was empty and I was trying to break into my mother's house like that was something people do.

CHAPTER TWELVE

TEDDY

FUCK THIS FUCKING SHIT. I decided to have all my hair cut off. All of it. I made Cheryl shave my head and I think my dad was pretty pissed off. She did a crap job with her fucked-up hand. Who comes home covered in blood mumbling about an accident with a grocery cart? My father told her she needed stitches and she looked at him like he was from Mars, then wrapped her hand in gauze and Band-Aids.

My father wanted me to get a proper cut at the barber, but this way it was questionable what injuries I really sustained in the crash. I had a scar on the back of my head from when I was a kid and now it was there for everyone to see and to question. It was an indictment of my father in a way that felt good. He was acting weird even when he was being supportive. It pissed me off that he looked at me as some kind of weakling that he had to prop up and cheerlead. Where was he before?

I met with Richard Shepard and he said that unfortunately they had to fill the position with someone else. The workflow could not stop while I was in recovery. Also, no one wanted a crippled person trying to sell them health products. He didn't say that, but I knew that's what he meant when he told me spending time on my recovery was the most important thing right now. How would I encourage trust if I was trying to be discreet about my arm? How would I bring anyone into an equation of success when I myself might be a fucked-up gimp forever? I didn't see what the opportunities were anymore. I only saw fucked-up situations and obstacles. My father wasn't hearing me and wanted me to go on other interviews. He wanted me to hit the ground running. He wanted my survival skills to kick in. It was an arm, I still had another one, and he had seen plenty of guys out in the field with malformed hands and other unfortunate body parts. They weren't the best sales guys, but their take-home was pretty okay. I could still do this. Besides, maybe my arm would heal and I could be like new.

I wasn't hired anywhere. My father pretended to be surprised. My doctor told me to focus on physical therapy. I was focused on the fact that I couldn't even grab my cock with my right hand anymore. After the latest sad display of trying to squeeze a rubber ball, I sat on the couch in the living room watching guys and girls my age engage in feats of strength on TV. Rope pulls and muddy scrambles up wood-plank walls and fumbled runs through tire obstacle courses for the hope of winning one hundred thousand dollars. Even the women looked tough with their muscled arms and braided pigtails. They were shouting at the guys to run faster, hand them the flag quicker; they muscled one another out of the way trying to reach the goal. The women had painted stripes on their faces to look savage and their faces contorted with each scream of "GO."

I had an erection and looked around to see if Cheryl or my dad were around. I stared at the girls on TV, covered in dirt and sweat, as they jumped up and down cheering. I sat on my left hand and waited for the pins and needles and then took out my penis and started to rub. I wanted to feel like it was someone else, not me, tugging. "The Mysterious Stranger," we called it when we were younger, laughing.

"I'm dying for a drink. What time is it?" I heard Cheryl say from the other room.

I panicked and stopped, slid down on the couch and tucked my penis into my waistband, praying for it to go down.

"I didn't even know you were in here," Cheryl said, standing over me, smiling. "So, is it too early for a cocktail or not?"

"I don't know."

I wanted to get up and run upstairs, but I was afraid she'd see my erection. I turned the channel away from the competition and onto cooking and heard her say, "She makes the best quiche," like she was sad about it.

"JESUS!"

"What's wrong? Are you in pain?"

I didn't know how to get rid of her and her concern, so I said, "Just leave me alone, okay?"

Her face fell and I instantly felt bad. She was the only one who gave a shit about me around here and I tried to be nice when she doted on me.

"Well, I'm going to have a drink with or without you," she said.

"Are you ever going to take that thing off?" I asked, pointing to her makeshift hand wrapping.

"When it heals," she said.

I stared down at my hands, one burning with pain and the other blank. It was the first time since the accident that I had gotten an erection and now it was gone.

"I'll have a beer, I guess," I said.

She smiled at me like she thought we were bonding or something.

CHAPTER THIRTEEN

CHERYL

I REFUSED TO GO to the doctor about my hand even after Jeffrey showed me pictures of what tetanus could do to a person. I didn't know what else to say but that I had been grocery shopping and cut my hand on a jagged part of the cart. Teddy asked where the groceries were. Jeffrey wanted to call the store and demand they pay for my doctor's visit. I told him I wasn't going anyway, and for a while the wound festered, but I got it under control. I stared at the length of the cut, how it split the life line in my palm in two.

Teddy said, "I guess we're all fucked up now." Jeffrey was not amused. The mail had piled up while Teddy was in the hospital, so when workers started erecting a large white fence all around us, I couldn't believe it was happening so soon.

The workers said they were just doing what they were told and the association told me to check the letter they had sent.

I found it in the pile. It didn't mention anything about apprehending a fisherman in front of our house or about his crying child.

Or even mention Teddy's accident directly. I watched the workers build the white picket fence blocking access to the ocean and knew that once they were finished they wouldn't be allowed in, either. They worked furiously. Even from here I could tell it was plastic by its sheen in the sun. Everyone was on high alert and, as the letter requested, being vigilant. The neighborhood had never felt more unsafe and we were all eyeing one another as potential threats.

I looked down and realized I was still holding the letter in my hand and carefully reread it. *Brutal attack on the nature trail.* It felt so far away now, so impossible. I had hardly seen Steven since that day, just momentary glimpses while Fran ushered him off in the family SUV. I couldn't see anything through their tinted windows, but I let Steven see me. When they passed today, I stood in the driveway defiantly. Fran gave a sad, small wave. As if her plight was worse than the rest of ours.

Jeffrey was away on business, somewhere in Omaha, he said. He had been gone for two days and I was alone with Teddy, administering his pain medication, unsure how much was too much. He kept asking for more and I didn't want to deny him. I was the cause, after all. Jeffrey let me know that with his back turned toward me in bed. I was surprised he hadn't moved to the other room. I was waiting to find out how long I had here, or if he had been quietly trying to forgive me.

I walked around the house and toward the ocean and stared out. Storm clouds. Hurricane season was all they were talking about on the news lately. They wanted us to have provisions and go bags and piles of just-in-case sandbags. When black clouds would roll in and the pool would be closed on account of lightning nearby, the harbor master would sound an alarm, something even louder for the boats. A cannon would be shot and we knew it was time to come home. That's what I was waiting for now—a cannon to sound, something to tell us not to leave our homes, but it never came. The sky was too blue.

Jeffrey had told me to take Teddy around to the club. "We can't stop living."

Teddy had hardly looked up from the television when Jeffrey said it. He'd absently clicked through the channels with his good arm, his other in a black sling.

I had assured Jeffrey that we would go.

"Cheryl?"

I turned around. Teddy was standing in the glass doorway, watching me weed the garden.

"Do you need help?" he asked.

"I think I'm almost finished," I said.

He stepped out onto the slate walk and closer to the bushes where I was weeding. "What are they doing over there?" he said.

I stared at the workers and said, "Building a fence."

"Who're they trying to keep out this time?" he asked.

"Everyone," I said.

He looked out at the islands, at the giant looming Tudors, and sighed. "I miss sailing," he said.

"I can imagine," I said.

"Can you? Really? I don't think you know what it's like to not be able to do something."

"How do you know?" I asked.

I looked up and he was pointing to his arm. He said, "Are you serious?"

"Point taken."

It was the most we had spoken in years, I think, and it was almost nice. I pulled at the weeds with more fury, trying to keep the peonies from falling over. He sat down on a lawn chair, tapping his fingers on the glass dining table we had out here.

"So I screwed things up for you and my dad, huh?"

"Screwed them up how?"

"I'm the rotting anchor."

"The rot has been there a long time," I said.

"You don't have to talk about it," he said, and I knew he didn't want to be the shoulder.

"How's your arm?" I asked.

"Fucked up."

I put my hand on my hip, trying to be stern.

"I don't know. It doesn't work," he said.

"It will," I said.

"You're always the optimist, Cheryl. How do you do it?"

"I fooled you, too?" I said, smiling.

"No, not at all. I was being sarcastic," he said.

We looked at each other and I wanted him to know the truth of things before he got any older. Like, one day you will love someone and then it will just go away and you will need to choose to hang on or you won't and you will never know which choice was the better one.

"Do you like birds?" I asked.

"Sometimes," he said.

"Do you want to take a walk with me on the nature trail?"

"Isn't that where Steven was attacked?" he asked.

I kept wanting to go back, to see my secrets. Just not alone.

"He was alone" is what I said instead.

"I don't know what a middle-aged lady and a kid with a gimp arm are going to do to fend anyone off."

I'm not middle aged, I thought.

"Do you know cranes have about ten different ways of showing that they're being threatened?" I asked.

Teddy started laughing. "No, I had no idea."

"Well, they do," I said. "So if we have a few less than that we'll still be fine."

"Maybe the cranes can go after anyone who tries to attack us."

"No one's going to do anything to us," I said.

"I'm sick of being in the house, anyway," he said. "Any other bird facts? Any of those birds out there cannibals?"

"Only when provoked, I think," I said, smiling, and he smiled, too.

I was careful to avoid the area around the tennis courts, so we walked along the seawall. They were spray-painting private property along the cement as we walked through and I stepped off the seawall to walk on the neighboring lawns instead.

"When is summer going to be over? I want all these people to go away," he said.

I looked around at the sprawling clubhouse, the pool overlooking the boats. We were walking slowly, listening to the bells on the boats jingle as the waves jostled the hulls. Kids screamed as they jumped in the pool and I looked at Teddy's arm.

"Their fun depresses the shit out of me," Teddy said.

"They're not really having fun. They just want everyone else to think they are."

"That's profound, Cheryl."

I could always count on Teddy to be an asshole.

He had a right to be angry because no one was sure when he'd be able to use his arm again, if ever. Rob Girardi was an orthopedic surgeon and he'd agreed to look at Teddy's arm. He'd said the same thing: "No telling right now."

I wanted him to get better because he was working so hard. Trying the smallest movements, electric stimuli, massaging the nerves back to life. The changes were imperceptible.

The reeds and marsh grass were bending into the trail, encasing us as we walked. Everything seemed to have grown so much in a short time and it felt so claustrophobic.

"You okay?" Teddy said. He reached out with his good hand and I knew it was awkward for him.

"Fine. I'm fine. I love it here," I said.

"Yeah, it sucks you've been stuck in the house with me instead of being able to come here."

"Don't feel bad about it. I needed a break anyway," I said.

"You probably know all these birds' names, right?" Teddy asked.

"Sometimes there are surprises."

The reeds swayed in the breeze and it seemed like nothing bad could happen here, even though something already had. I felt like I was recapturing my sanctuary. "So, what's that one called?" he asked.

I looked around, trying to find what he was talking about. Then I thought I picked up the sound of whistling and felt the need to flee.

He pointed to the sky as a small bird flitted overhead.

"That's a common sparrow," I said.

"That's cool," he said. "I thought it was something better."

I was looking at the base of the reeds, trying to find my binoculars discreetly.

"What are you looking for? Nests?"

"Dog shit, actually. There's an ordinance about it and no one cares."

"You can't police the world, Cheryl." He looked at me and smiled, trying to make a joke.

"I know. I know. I'm working on it."

We came upon an opening in the reeds and the cattails and I exhaled for the first time since we started on the trail. The sun was glorious and the tide was high; the inlet into the marsh was thick with birds—tufted ducks, the magnificent black-bellied plover, egrets, herons—they just went on with it all as if nothing had happened here. They ducked in and out of the water looking for food as the crabs slowly inched through the mud and the small, black mussels shot thin streams of water into the air in concert.

We kept on, falling back into the maze of reeds after the temporary breadth of space. We walked toward a bend in the reeds, everything ahead of us obscured.

A man came ripping through on a bicycle and I jumped into Teddy and yelped.

"Jesus Christ, Cheryl!" Teddy yelled.

I pulled him out of the reeds.

"I'm sorry. I'm sorry," the man said.

"Watch where the hell you're going," I said. He was harmless, older, but it didn't matter.

"I didn't see anyone up ahead."

"It's a blind curve, so how could you?" I asked.

He jumped back on his bike and rode away, calling out sorry again but not wanting to get involved in our situation.

"Are you okay?" I asked.

"My shoes are a little wet, that's all."

"Maybe we should head back."

"It was a dude on a bike, Cheryl."

"I know, I know," I said.

"We have to get it together. Get healthy."

He pointed to my hand. I was down to a few waterproof Band-Aids and a twice-daily application of Neosporin.

"Maybe we should start juicing," I said.

"That's not going to help us at all," he said. "We can't just be shut-ins. We're going to end up on an episode of fucking *Hoarders* or whatever."

"I see you more as a guest on *Intervention*," I said.

"That's not even okay to say," Teddy said.

I put my arm around him and told him I was joking. "You're doing a great job," I said.

"I'm saying, we shit the bed, you know?"

"I don't even know what that means," I said.

"You're scared of a guy on a bicycle wearing tights," he said. "In tights."

"It could be worse."

A week of rain came and I only got out of bed to give Teddy his pills and take him to his physical therapy appointments near the hospital. It was a tropical depression, nothing major. Together, Teddy and I would try to do the exercises they said he would respond to. He wasn't seeing results, though, and I saw him giving up hope. I was, too. Since the accident Jeffrey had tried to steer clear of me, no matter what attempts I made. I wasn't going for walks anymore, just sitting on the patio chair watching the water and the sun rise when the rain would pause from the safety of the yard.

"Is there any food?" Teddy yelled from the sofa. I opened the fridge and it was filled wall to wall with food. I asked him what he wanted and he only grumbled, saying he wasn't sure.

"Work with me," I said. "What are you in the mood for?"

"I don't know, really. Surprise me," he said. I wanted to drop him off in front of a Wendy's.

I had been taking care of him and I had come to loathe any talk of food. *What's for dinner?* was the worst. There wasn't a single day when I cared about what was for dinner, but for Teddy and Jeffrey it seemed like that was all they could think about. With Teddy here, suddenly there had to be a routine. He was always hungry. I couldn't toss a bowl of cereal toward Teddy, either, it had to be a meal. Jeffrey needed at least one vegetable. Teddy asked me if I wanted some more cookbooks to vary things up. Things were becoming unbearable. Teddy and I ordered pizza and watched the men build the fence outside. They didn't stop for the rain. Watching them work became an obsession of mine. It almost looked like they were trying to keep the water out, like it would never reach us here. I worried about the broken window at my mother's house, of water pouring into the broken window and filling the house with mold.

I decided to cut up the club directory and only keep fortune-cookie-size slips of printed phone numbers in a drawer by my bedside. I blocked my number and started my calls. A woman picked up and sounded impatient. I hung up quickly, apologizing for calling the wrong number. The second was a young boy. I hesitated and then just hung up on him without a word.

On the third call, a man picked up and I didn't recognize his voice. It could have been anyone. I made my voice sound youthful and said "Hello" like it wasn't even a question.

He sounded impatient on the phone and for a moment I considered hanging up.

"How are you feeling?" I tried to sound familiar, to make him unsure.

"Fine. Who is this?"

"Whoever you want me to be," I said, and waited for the silence.

"Look, I'm kind of in a rush," he said. Then, "Can you call back?"

I stared down at the slip with the number and said, "I'm not sure."

"Please."

I thought about it. "Who do you want me to be?" I asked.

"I'm not sure yet."

I hung up the phone and crumpled the paper and threw it in the garbage. I stuck my hand in the drawer and pulled out another fortune and dialed.

"Hello?"

"Hi," I said.

"Hello."

The voice sounded middle-aged. It didn't have the crackle of age or the squeak of youth. I asked him how he was doing and he said he was just fine. He sounded like he was waiting for me to start selling him something. His polite silence worried me. The aggressive ones were usually more interested in talking to me. Something about his voice seemed familiar, but I decided to ignore that. I decided to head him off.

"I'm not trying to sell you anything," I said. And then, after a silence, I asked him what was wrong.

"Well, right now, I'm not sure who I'm talking to and you won't tell me who you are or why you're calling," he said.

"You didn't ask who this was," I said.

I had to be careful here because he could think I was teasing him and some men didn't like to be teased.

"Who is this?" he asked.

"Whoever you want me to be."

"Is that so?"

"Yes," I whispered.

He cleared his throat and then it sounded like he was moving to sit down, get comfortable. "There are so many options," he said.

"Try me," I said.

He let out a sigh and said, "I just don't know."

I heard Teddy making his way to the bathroom and thought about hanging up. This man wasn't progressing fast enough. He was probably Kirk from down the street, a bad golfer and a mediocre husband.

"Why don't you just say a name?"

I knew Teddy wouldn't come in or even knock on my door when it was closed. I don't think he liked coming into the bedroom where his father and I slept, even when we weren't at home.

"How about Marilyn?" I played my Marilyn for him and he seemed to like it.

"Sing me happy birthday." He laughed.

"Is it your birthday?"

"Well, no," he said, so I told him I couldn't.

"You're not very nice to me," he said.

"I could be," I said.

"What do I have to do to get that?" he said, getting into things now.

"I haven't decided yet."

I looked out the window. The men were hard at work on the fence outside; they were only two houses away.

"Do you like yourself?" I asked, really curious.

It took him off guard. I think he was waiting for me to ask him something more pleasant, sexual.

"I like myself all right."

"Good," I whispered. "I thought you might be bad."

He gave a high-octave laugh and then said, "Is this a test? A trick to get me to say something bad so you can tell my wife?"

"I don't even know who your wife is," I said. I wasn't lying.

"What are you wearing?" he asked.

"Nothing," I said, looking down at my plaid nightgown.

He said, "Wow," and nearly choked on the word. "So you think you're naughty?" he asked.

I nearly giggled. I was getting into it again. Then I heard "Daddy!" yelled in the background.

"I have to go," he said. And then he was gone.

I closed the drawer full of scraps and threw away this man's phone number. I had forgotten how to be sexual and I cringed thinking that these people might be embarrassed for me. What was I even doing?

I went into Jeffrey's office and stared at his computer. My skin began to tingle as I walked over, sat down, and turned it on. I opened his web browser and looked at the history. It was blank. He'd erased it, which made me realize that he knew I was checking. I knew there would be something somewhere he was directing all his attention to. And then, after clicking around, I found it in his download folder: Luz_hotfucking.mov.

I trembled as I opened the folder. A video popped up and it was pixelated and grainy. A young woman waited on a dirty mattress and spread her legs wide. She stared at the man holding the camera and tried to smile. She was young, brown-haired and light-skinned. She looked oddly familiar. It was impossible that I'd seen her before, wasn't it? The cameraman bent her over and started to have sex with her. She turned around and looked like she was crying. Then I knew why she looked familiar. She looked like the young girl crying for her father, the man on the ground with his fishing poles. I fumbled at the keyboard, trying to shut the video off. I didn't know how, so I just slammed the screen down shut. The sound was muffled but still on and I could hear her moans and screams.

And then a man's voice said, "Say you want it."

I sat there for a moment. He kept saying, "Say you want it." Then a small voice with a thick accent said, "I want it," over and over again.

I opened the laptop and he was shoving his penis into her mouth. I paused the video and looked at her face. Tears were frozen in a stream down her swollen cheeks. This is what Jeffrey wanted? He was trying to take so many things from her.

I minimized the window and opened another window. I stared at my mother's ramshackle house. We didn't have the internet back then. The sex happened skin on skin. There were no affairs with computer screens or disinterest because someone was waiting to video chat with wide-open legs. I had seen it all and ignored it for the good of us. It was part of the deal and it's what made him the marrying kind, straying without hurting anyone. No one told me about the things that happened to all of us.

I stared at my mother's dark house. How could I know so much and know nothing?

CHAPTER FOURTEEN

TEDDY

I WAS PRETTY SURE that Cheryl was chowing down on my pills. Some days she was nearly catatonic and it creeped me out. I couldn't sleep and I found her sitting outside wrapped in a blanket staring at the dark skyline. I wasn't sure if it was because she missed my dad or what. He was going away more and more now and I didn't really think he had had a sudden uptick in business trips. I think he just needed to get away from both of us. My dad has never been good at taking care of people. It just wasn't his thing. He couldn't take care of my mom and he couldn't take care of himself. If Cheryl wasn't careful he'd leave her, too. I almost felt bad for her because she didn't see the patterns like I did. She had no context; she didn't know that this is how it started with him. Emergency trips, longer trips, extended trips. I need to bring my golf clubs along because that's where we have meetings. When they first got together, he used to take her along because that's what wives like her are for—showing off and saying I win. She might not be a great conversationalist, but she was really nice to look at. Don't you feel bad about your wife with the wide hips? It was all mind-control shit. It was how he got the top-shelf accounts. No one wanted a middle-aged loser handling their account; they wanted someone who could attract a new young wife and knew the value in that kind of play. Strategic life plays. She looked like she had aged since the accident.

"Have you slept at all?" I asked as I stepped outside. She turned around, startled, and said, "A little."

I looked up. Every star in the sky was lit up like white pinpricks. It was amazing.

"It's beautiful."

"Isn't it?" she asked, shaking her head. "How could you ever leave a place like this?"

I sat down beside her and we watched the sky turn gray and the water light up. I was never going to be able to sail again. *Screw this, Teddy. No dark thoughts; we went over this.* I wanted to know when my father would be back. Cheryl didn't seem to have any answers.

"Teddy?" she asked after a moment.

"Yeah," I answered.

"Why hasn't anyone come to visit you?"

I thought at least Pauline would come, but no, it was just me and Cheryl now. The pariahs of Little Neck Cove. I wasn't sure what she had done to deserve it, but me? Me, it was well deserved.

"I don't know."

The pain was acting up in my arm again. So now finally I had all the pills I ever wanted, and I didn't even really want them anymore. The irony wasn't lost on me. I wanted to be awake and feeling things again. Flipping your car will do that, I guess. Isn't that what people say: I had a terrible accident, almost died, and now I wanted to live?

Well, I didn't almost die. It's not like I drove off a cliff or anything. I just plowed into the net of the tennis courts upside down.

Being unable to move my arm indefinitely seemed
sive outcome to something so small, right? I didn't reall
anymore. No matter how hard I tried I couldn't get n
wiggle. Something I could do so easily before, I couldn'
all now. My brain couldn't will things into existence anym

It pissed me off. It really did. I'm not saying that it w.
deal. I ruined the tennis season for all these bastards. I was
less. I think I made my father cry.

These were all undesirable outcomes. It just didn't seem to
was all that I was saying. They put me on a morphine drip f
a week at the hospital while they checked things and opened t
and made sure of things. I saw things then. I mean visions. Tl
that made me uncomfortable. Cheryl needed her own dose, b
wasn't about to share my pile. I counted them every few days. I j
really liked to see them poured out on the counter, rounded ed;
like Chiclets, to make sure they were still there. Old habits and ;
that.

"Look how pretty the water is just before the sun rises," Cheryl
said.

It was. I looked up at the fading stars and understood why Cheryl
didn't feel the urge to sleep. How could you miss all this? I held my
phone up to the sky and Cheryl asked me what I was doing.

"I have this thing on my phone that tells you what you're looking
at," I said.

She smiled at me, then looked up at the sky and said, "Big Dipper,
Little Dipper, Orion, Gemini, Mars, Venus . . ."

She pointed and recited and I was amazed. She put her arm down
and said, "Good memory from college astronomy."

"You're making me wish I'd paid better attention in class," I said.

"We'll see Mercury better around sunrise," she said, and I put my
phone down and stared up at the sky.

"I fucked up, I think," I said.

"Which part?"

"Life, school, all of it," I said.

"Who hasn't?" Cheryl asked, still staring up at the sky.

I didn't want to hear that no one knew what they were doing.

"It's going to be a perfect day to be out on the water," she said a few minutes later. "Let's go sailing."

"You don't even know how to sail," I reminded her.

"You do."

I kinda thought she was suggesting it to piss my dad off because he had given up early trying to take her sailing. She didn't move fast enough to be of any help. He said he needed another sailor, not someone who just wanted to tan on a boat.

I told her I couldn't do it one-handed and she said she would help. She said, "We have the whole day ahead of us."

She had a point. Days dragged on in this house and the only excitement in my life lately was doctor's visits and being jabbed by needles and other medical instruments.

"Maybe go to sleep for a while and then we'll go," I said.

She looked at me and smiled and said she would.

Hours later, I woke up in my bed, the sun hot and bright. I got up and opened my drawers looking for clothes that were easy to put on, clothes that didn't require buttons or zippers or anything like that. I waited for her downstairs and when she came down, she looked like good old Cheryl. She wore superbright colors, like she really wanted to be noticed. Today she had on neon-green shorts and a pink top. I didn't even want to ask what had inspired this look.

We walked on the wall in defiance of the No Trespassing signs and headed toward Joanne in her slip.

Cheryl helped me pick off the seashells this time and she kept some and threw the rest of them away. She would leave seashells in the yard

and my father would go nuts saying they got caught up in the mower. Cheryl didn't care. She said she liked the way they looked with her flowers. I said, "Are you going to put those in the yard, too?" and she said, "Maybe."

Lately, everything that came out of her mouth sounded cryptic.

I told her how to start the motor because I needed two hands to do it. She pulled the string a few times really wimpy, so I told her to really pull and on that last turn she pulled with all this anger and exhaust spilled out from the motor. We were ready to go.

"Are you sure you want to do this?" I asked, really trying to say *Can you handle this on your own, because I'm kinda scared that I won't be able to jump in to help if shit goes awry.*

She said, "I want to learn," and we set off together as she kept saying, "This is going to be fun."

Trapped on a sailboat together heading out to the Long Island Sound and I started thinking that maybe this was nuts. What were we going to talk about for all these hours? Maybe she'd be okay with staying silent except for when we had to move the sail. Because this was feeling kind of therapeutic right now and my physical therapist had told me to find therapeutic things to do.

I put my bad hand in the water, letting it drag off the side to try to feel things, while staring down into the water.

The wind changed direction and I told her to change the tack. I had to keep it simple, even though I'd explained some sailing terms to her when we got on the boat. It was almost hilarious, Cheryl and I sailing.

CHAPTER FIFTEEN

CHERYL

TO TAKE THE BOAT out without even asking, without even mentioning to Jeffrey what we were doing, felt like we were making a run for it. The view of the homes from the water was something to marvel at. A row of muted tones faced out, with the slimmest breaks in between each house, the lawns blending into each other in one manicured line. Nearly every home had a flagpole with not only the American flag flying, but small, narrow yacht club flags as well. No one shied away from their nautical convictions here. When Teddy and I boarded Jeffrey's boat, I tried to ignore the Joanne in big letters staring back at me. Jeffrey and Teddy's grief was an infection that would not budge. The fear of loss kept them from really trying with anyone else. I had taken that burden on myself, though. I was in the shadow of a dead woman, a flawed, beloved woman here. There were remnants of her everywhere: long-forgotten boxes in the garage, half-finished airplane bottles of liquor jammed in the back of drawers and cabinets, a monogrammed washcloth stuffed behind our daily-use set in the linen closet. She was everywhere and nowhere.

Sometimes I wondered if things would have been different if I had met Jeffrey well after her death rather than having it infect our marriage during its honeymoon stage. It made us feel guilty for our happiness. It made us feel watched and scrutinized.

"Tack left."

We both leaned down under the sail, and I swung it over us, and we sat on the opposite side.

"You're much easier to sail with than your father."

"Oh yeah, he takes the joy out of anything."

"He's not all bad."

"Say it like you mean it, Cheryl," Teddy said, laughing.

We stared at the waves, the water bright and shiny in the distance, and the islands that dotted the landscape.

"Where do you want to go?" I asked.

We both stared out at the stretch of water and then Teddy said, "I don't know. Far away. As far as we can go."

I looked down deep into the water and wondered what was under us, the murky gray-green water. The jellyfish weren't out yet, floating like implants along the face of the water. It was still safe to put your hands in.

"Whatever you want."

He leaned his hand into the water and we sailed forward and I felt in control for the first time in a long time. We sailed away from the houses, the long fence being erected, Lori's sand, and the club.

"What a beautiful day. We're so lucky," I said.

"Speak for yourself," Teddy said. "Speak for yourself." He stared down at his hand as the water slid through his fingers.

"I'm sorry," I said.

"It's not your fault," he said. "It's just the way things happen sometimes." If I don't say anything now, I thought, he might never know. "Did you ever sail before you met my dad?" he asked.

"Once, and we capsized," I said.

"That's the worst. My dad used to capsize us just to see how well I fared under pressure."

"How could your mother let him do that?"

Teddy laughed and said, "She was always jumping around the shore, pissed. She loved to sail, though. That's where I get it from. That, and you know, she thought it was a super important part of networking. Starting in kindergarten with golf and yachting and private schools and shit. Get in line with your kind."

"I wish I'd had that when I was your age," I said.

"You grew up here, too, didn't you?" he asked.

I told him that I had grown up not far from here, in the northeastern corner of the state, where farms and chickens outnumbered people. It was amazing that a few dozen miles could create such a distance in lives. The shoreline was a dream and in the summers we'd pack up and drive to Hammonasset, the one public beach we could find, and pretend we belonged by the water. We'd stare down the shore toward the private beaches and wonder how you could own something like that, the sand and the water.

He asked me who the "we" was and, trapped on this boat, I felt like I was telling him too much.

He pressed me further, asking where they were. I didn't know, I told him. We had lost touch. It was not untrue. I hadn't spoken to my sisters in so many years. We had detached from one another somewhere along the way and never thought to realign, come together, remember who we were or where we came from. We had been too busy surviving to feel any sense of closeness from our shared history. I wondered if they thought about my mother, reached out to her, or forgave her for anything.

"All this," Teddy said, waving toward the houses and club, "doesn't amount to much if you don't care or try, you know? You gotta want to put on your armor of seersucker, get out there, and make the connections. I don't really care, so the tennis lessons and sending me to Kent and Dartmouth were probably worthless."

"Those things can never be taken away from you. You're privileged."

Teddy looked at me with disgust and said, "If I was, I'd still have my mom."

We sat quietly and stared out at the water.

"I'm sorry," he said after a while.

"I'm sorry you don't have your mother anymore," I said.

The boat hit a wave and rocked violently. Teddy scrambled to grab hold of the loose ropes of the mast.

"It's fine," he said. "Calm down. Tack right."

I leaped forward, barely missing Teddy as we slid under the mast.

"You did a beautiful job cleaning the boat, Teddy," I said, fingering the top of the letter J on the back of the boat.

"She would be sick to see how he's let it go to waste."

"He just can't look at it," I said.

"Then sell it." He turned toward me and said it again, "Then sell it."

"He knows you would never speak to him again."

"Let it go or keep it and take care of it. Don't make her an eyesore. Something to be whispered about and mocked. Fuck him."

"He's trying," I said.

"Yeah, with you, me, and everyone. Really well. Where the fuck is he, anyway?"

"Grief hits people in different ways," I said.

"How long is it supposed to feel like this? Forever? I can't take *forever*."

I didn't know how to answer him. Jeffrey couldn't shake it, I could see it. The guilt radiated off him. *She wouldn't be drinking so much all the time if . . .* It always came back to if they had just been better. The fact that she died so visibly and tragically—her drunken fall off the docks in the middle of the night—brought the community together and kept me out. They martyred her without all the facts. Sometimes I wondered if it was a conscious decision or the accident everyone believed it to be. I never expected Jeffrey to get over his love for her. Or maybe I did, at first, naively.

I stared at Teddy's pained face. I could see that his rush to numb himself had a higher purpose and I couldn't blame him. I didn't want him to see me as a mother; I knew that was not the way things worked.

The question of a child of my own was taken care of quickly with Jeffrey. He simply could not have another, his choice was irreversible, and came well before me. I didn't know until I was in my late thirties, when I saw the smiling mothers, doting on their children, and panic hit because my choice would soon be gone. That's when he told me, when I had decided that I had a lack to fill.

"I'm sorry," Teddy said.

He stared off into the water and we watched motorboats in the distance. I asked him if his friends still came home in the summer, if he told anyone about the accident. He stared at me blankly.

"We have different interests."

He had spent most of his time in private school, so he hadn't roamed the streets like the boys from the neighborhood, who strayed from the public school, but they had all grown up together, so I thought there would be some kind of lingering affection.

He said, "What do they want with a cripple, anyway?"

We sat in silence for a while, until I said, "Don't say 'cripple.'"

"What's the polite way of saying it?"

"I don't know, but just not that."

"We're not PC here, remember?" he said.

"Don't put yourself down is all."

"What now?" he asked.

"You get better." I wanted to believe that my actions would not be irreversible.

"No, I mean, where do you want to go?" he asked.

"Should we sail home?"

"Let's keep going. I don't want to go back," he said.

I held on to the rope and kept the mast steady. We pressed on toward the horizon.

I had sunburn and windburn from sailing with Teddy all day. My back hurt from being hunched over for hours, keeping my attention on the flapping sail and sturdy mast. It was so freeing to be on the water, the only thing to guide us was a desire to be as far away from Little Neck Cove as possible, even if just for a little while. When we finally decided to turn around, neither of us anticipated how long it would take to sail back. The water felt endless and curled beneath us, sending the front of the boat jutting up and jerking. We oriented ourselves carefully on the boat and I was in control of this fast-moving vessel. When was the last time I could say that I had been in control? Now I understood why Teddy would spend endless hours on the boat, why he sometimes chose to drift. For a moment, you could feel no tethers to anything. You just had one distinct purpose—to keep yourself righted.

At home in front of the mirror, I thought about how close I was getting to fifty. A few more years I wouldn't notice passing. What then? Eye the young ones with more venom? I didn't want to feel this way anymore. I wanted to be the one to benefit from someone's youth. My face had always been a bit pudgy, and looking at myself now, I saw the kind of thin face I had dreamed about as a teenager. I didn't think I could possibly feel worse than my fourteen-year-old self, but here it was. I couldn't bounce back like I used to and it made me think about all the mistakes, the chances I didn't take, the changes I had been afraid to make. What was I going to do now? The biotin treatments I had purchased at the drugstore in town didn't seem to be working. Perhaps I should have bought the ones not on sale, the more expensive brand with the dark and serious packaging. I pretended my creams and jars were the expensive kind, so I could justify the money I was setting aside to send to my mother. I did more with less, so she could have the money. I was the closest child, the youngest daughter, and I was the one with the obligation.

How many times a day would I spend my time standing in the bathroom hoping to find someone better there? I opened the bathroom drawer and found lipsticks and shiny bottles of foundation and blush, and mountains of samples. Eye cream, face cream, serum, whitening toothpaste, samples of perfume ranging from exotic smells to ho-hum tuberose. I had slickly-decorated squares of shampoos and conditioners and hair mud masks. I hadn't touched any of them; I just kept them in piles in my drawer. There were small plastic bottles of lotions and shampoos from the hotels Jeffrey visited, piles of them. He had deposited them along with my samples and had slowly been using them, not buying his own shampoo in years. He lived out of these small bottles, even when he was at home.

It was a way of tracking him, making sure he was actually where he said he was. After each trip he'd pull his small black carrying case out of his luggage and tug at the collection of plastic bottles and arrange them in my drawer. Some he placed inside the shower, in a line around the edges of the square shower. I made a space for the plastic bottles that he would soon be depositing but didn't throw away my own, even though some had started to leak and I'm sure it upset him.

I moved my hand deeper into the drawer and pulled out Teddy's diazepam and fondled the bottle, touching the orange bottle with the paper label almost lovingly. I hadn't felt the pull or strength of something this strong since I first met Jeffrey and couldn't stand to be away from him.

I put it back for later, deep inside, so Teddy wouldn't find it.

But that didn't work at all, so I took one and then I put the bottle back. Just one.

I looked at myself, at the makeup I had previously applied, smoothed out my outfit, and waited for the pill to take effect. It was small and unassuming in my palm when I was holding it, like candy. They even had them in pastel colors to make them more pleasant to look at. I thought that Teddy probably had other ways of getting stronger medicine than diazepam, so everything was fine.

As soon as the pill began to work, I would be ready to go to the clambake and face them. Teddy was going, too.

"You ready?" Teddy asked, walking into the bathroom.

I looked at him, madras plaid shorts, boat shoes that needed to be thrown away, and a long-sleeve button-down shirt, I assume to cover his arm. He'd wandered around the house for weeks in his gym shorts, so this was a significant change.

"I think so," I said. "You look good."

"Thanks, this is me trying."

"I can tell," I said. "Do I look scared?"

"What are you so scared about? You didn't do thousands of dollars of damage to the place," Teddy said.

"No one remembers that anymore. Not since Nora's ex-husband got drunk and naked and jumped into the pool," I said.

"That's true. At least I keep my dick in my pants in front of other people."

He scratched at his head with his good arm and laughed. I stared at his limp arm and he caught me staring at it and turned away and I heard his shoes walking quickly down the hall. I looked at myself and applied blush once again. The pill was working; I didn't care about anything, really.

Teddy and I walked along the seawall, once again ignoring the signs that said no trespassing in bright red.

"Soon the whole horizon line will be covered with these signs," he said.

"They want to make sure there's no room for discussion," I said.

He walked in front of me and dangled his arm down next to him. I stared at the long scar on the back of his head and wondered where he'd gotten it, if Jeffrey had hit him. He was certainly capable of it. I saw the scar for the first time when I shaved Teddy's head but didn't think to ask about the jagged divide between his head and neck. Teddy turned to look, almost like he was making sure I was still there. I smiled at him, tried to radiate some kind of bravery for him. A crowd of seersucker had formed on the lawn and we both hesitated for a moment. Finally, he jumped off the seawall and opened the latch on the gate, which had its own tasteful sign reiterating that no one should be here.

"Are you sure about this?" he asked.

"No, are you?"

"Fuck no," he said.

Teddy slowed and fell back, walking next to me. I was trying to get oriented, but I was moving slowly because of the diazepam.

"There's Cronin," he said.

I didn't want to turn around and face Steven, but I finally did.

"Man, he's fucked up," Teddy said.

There was a crisscross of scars over Steven's face, his cheek still swollen. *Maybe* he *wanted it*, I thought. Maybe he was asking for it. I could see his eyes and I had not gotten the memory of them wrong. He watched me now like I had wanted him to before. I wanted to know what he was thinking. If he hated me. I felt ashamed for even caring.

Someone grabbed me from behind and I nearly jumped a foot. I turned and it was Tuck.

"Oh, come on. You could hear me coming," he said, smiling.

Teddy looked at us both, uneasy, and walked away.

Tuck leaned in close. "So, have you found out yet?"

"What?"

"What's wrong with you?" he asked. "Are you high? Do you need to sit down?"

I made a face and shook my head while he laughed.

"Even if I were high, I'd never tell you," I said.

"I can keep a secret. What's wrong?"

"Do you want the short list or the long one?" I asked.

"Whichever is more heartbreaking," he said, winking at me.

"Gee, I don't know, that one's kinda long."

He leaned in close and I could smell him—salt water and stale beer.

"You wanna hear something fucked up?"

"I don't know," I said.

"Someone called me and talked dirty to me last night," he said, laughing.

"No," I said, backing away.

"I know, right? Sixteen-year-old self is back in action."

"Why don't you just hang up the phone?"

"I kinda like it." He smiled again. I made a face and he continued, "I pretend it's my wife."

"Yeah, right."

"It's true. Maybe I'm going to ask her to start calling me and talking to me. Or sexting."

"Tuck, god."

"Did I cross a line? Are you uncomfortable?"

I was absolutely mortified at the thought that he might know it was me. But if he did, he didn't let on.

"I don't care about the sex you have with your wife."

"Gotta keep it fresh," he said.

"At least you're not looking around at them."

I waved toward the young girls strutting around in eyelet dresses, playing prim for their parents.

"Been there, done that," Tuck said.

I looked at him in disgust.

"I briefly taught at a boarding school. That's where I met my wife," he said.

"Jesus Christ."

"I'm joking," he said and winked at me. "Lighten up. Sex is fun."

"I wouldn't know anymore."

Tuck said, "See, that shocks me. You gotta do it to remember you're not alone."

I watched as he sauntered away and pulled his bike out of the bushes. He was definitely drunk. I turned to see if anyone else was seeing what I was seeing but no one was paying any attention. He put his beer glass in a plastic cup holder on his handlebars and started pedaling away from the hum of conversation. I felt a flash of envy. His wife was one of the lucky ones.

"Oh, Cheryl, it's been ages!"

I turned around to see Lori in a low-cut tank top and capri pants. Her massive breasts were hanging down in the middle. I hadn't seen her much since she was yelling in the face of the old fisherman, shooing away his dog. She looked at me expectantly, searching my face to see if I would yell at her again. I didn't have the energy.

"How are you feeling? Can you believe it all?" she asked.

I didn't know what "all" she was talking about, so I just nodded.

"Funny that you'd come by here," she said.

"Why's that?" I knew what she was getting at, but I wanted her to say it.

"Well, under the circumstances," she said.

"What circumstances are those?"

"Oh, Cheryl." She clutched my arm and laughed nervously.

"Aren't you going to ask how he's doing?" I said.

"He's right over there! He looks wonderful," she said. "How's his arm?"

"He's working really hard," I answered.

I turned and looked at Teddy talking to Steven. They were both imperfect now, set aside from the rest of the men in pastel tones.

Steven looked past Teddy right at me. He stared at me with recognition. A waiter came by with some champagne and I quickly gulped a glass down.

"When the cat's away, the mouse will play, eh?"

"What?" I asked.

Lori was smirking at me, pointing at my empty glass.

"I was thirsty," I said.

"Fran's poor son. You can hardly stand to look at him," she said.

It was true. What I had done to him was permanent and visible to anyone who had looked at him. I had seen shadows of him since the incident, but this was the first time I was seeing him since he had healed. I didn't know how to feel. I had questioned what happened daily.

"Maybe he deserved it," I said.

"I don't think it was a fisherman at all," Lori said, raising an eyebrow. "I just don't believe it. Doesn't fit the pattern." She said "pattern" like she was some kind of detective. I asked her what pattern, but she wouldn't elaborate. Did she think someone was going around smashing people's faces?

"Do you think they happened before? Attacks?" I asked.

"You want insider information," she said, winking at me. "This community is not all peachy."

"I know. I'm not new," I said.

"Some people always feel a bit new, don't you think?" she said.

There were unfamiliar faces, younger women. They must have been new club members. They were young like I was when I first became a member. No jowls or loose neck skin. They would have them soon enough; I could already see their husbands peering around, looking at all those low-cut dresses, short skirts, and tanned, athletic legs. The still-vibrant wives chased after their children. What I noticed most was that none of those men looked at me like I was a possibility.

Coming here was a bad idea, I knew that for sure now. Lori lingered nearby but without more to talk about she faded back into a group of other women in the Tuesday-morning golf group. I heard them talking about handicaps and cheaters. I thought about handicaps, my own, and now Teddy's. I looked around for him and found him still talking to Steven.

How would Steven, with his scarred face, find women to take to the Captain's Lounge? Sit with his parents and his date, her skirt grazing her mid-thigh, her breasts that his father would look at. His face couldn't court that kind of girl anymore. Why hadn't he told someone? I wanted to corner him and shake him. Ask him what he was up to. There had to be a reason he was hiding this secret for us. I would think he would be afraid I could spill it all. Tell everyone what kind of person he was. He was acting like he had nothing to hide, like he was a victim.

I hurried toward the pool's locker rooms. I listened as the women laughed and washed their hands. They were talking about how good the calamari was this year and how all their kids wanted lobster for dinner but they hated cracking the shells for them.

If I had a child, I would crack the shell each time. They didn't know what they had. I sat on the toilet seat in a stall, waiting for the women to leave, but more came in. They were adjusting bras and fixing lipstick and if I came out of the stall now they would know that I had been eavesdropping.

One of them said, "God, I wish I had more than wine." When they finally stepped out of the bathroom, I came out of the stall. I didn't like seeing myself, hunched over, nearly cowering, and weak. These women didn't own me; they weren't better than me. They were just younger versions of me and soon enough they would be me.

CHAPTER SIXTEEN

TEDDY

I WAS STUCK TALKING to Steven Cronin. We were the two undesirable gimps and people kept giving us looks like we were ruining everyone's good time just by standing there and being in their line of vision.

I was tired of looking at Steven's fucked-up face and he kept asking me for drugs. He said he'd chowed through his painkillers and his mom was watching his intake on the second bottle. Times like this I wish my fucking arm worked, so I could deck him or something. I was going to make a list of the things I couldn't do anymore so that I would have goals to work toward. I scanned the crowd looking for Jill, but I couldn't find her anywhere.

Goal one—Kick someone's ass.

"So who fucked up your face?" I asked.

Steven blinked twice. "You heard," he said.

"Yeah, I heard. But I can see, too."

I didn't think there was some band of outsiders prowling the streets like everyone wanted to believe, and I told him so. Steven and I knew better.

Something had been bothering me lately. Cheryl was acting super weird and cagey and I couldn't even get out of her when Dad was supposed to come home. She acted like she didn't even know. Was that their setup now? He just left for weeks and she kept her mouth shut? She was going crazy from it. I did have to say, though, that she wasn't that bad to be around sometimes. Our little sailing trip was awkward at first, but then when we figured out that we didn't need to talk the whole time it all eased up. It was just good to be back out on the water again. And we'd started sitting in the yard together when we couldn't sleep and looking up at the night sky.

"No, man. I don't remember shit. One minute I'm just walking. The next I'm down on the ground and all I can feel is pain," he said.

"With your wang out?" I said. I knew I was pushing it, but he was a tool. A psycho, really.

"That was bullshit," he said.

"Pants around the ankles, I heard," I said.

"Listen, motherfucker." His face was getting red. If he hit me, I wouldn't be able to hit back. Everyone was always saying how cute Steven was when we were kids. He was just adorable. And so smart. Steven was just the smartest. He was a fucking genius. He was going to be someone, they all said. They could tell even when he was a kid. It radiated off him and I hated him for it. Cheryl came back out of the bathroom looking lost as hell. Steven stopped glaring at me long enough to look at her, watching her in a weird way.

"Hear what I said?" I said louder.

Steven looked back at me. "My junk was in my pants, asshole," he said and focused his attention back on Cheryl.

She took notice and looked startled, then started to rush toward home, leaving me alone. That wasn't part of the deal.

CHAPTER SEVENTEEN

CHERYL

I WALKED ALONG THE FENCE and tried to push it over. They had sealed the base in with concrete, so it was immovable. Why did they have to do it? I felt trapped, the water out of reach.

I looked out at the small docks near the rocky breakwater. Usually, the children's Sunfish sailboats were there all summer long, turned over and drying after long mornings and afternoons preparing for the end-of- summer race. Instead, the docks were empty and it felt strange.

I saw Tuck riding his bicycle down the road and waved him over.

"Haven't you seen enough of me tonight?"

"When you put it like that, yes," I said. I pointed out toward the water and asked, "Where are the boats? Are they being repaired?"

Tuck shook his head and took a sip from his thermos.

"Are you always drinking?" I asked.

He looked at me and said, "It's my relaxation hour."

I snorted.

"All you neighborhood ladies are so uptight, if you traveled with a beverage things like this wouldn't happen."

"I'm not like them," I said.

"You say that, but I haven't seen you prove it yet."

"When you're married to someone who's disinterested, all the other choices you have are frowned upon."

"Aw, come on now. I've just been teasing you all along. I don't want to be your confessor."

"You asshole," I said. "I thought you wanted me to feel alive."

"Less alone is what I said."

We looked at each other and knew we didn't want that from each other. He laughed and put his arm around me and I can't explain how good it felt to be touched. I wanted to be touched more than ever then.

He took his arm away and I could still feel the imprint of it as he waved his hand toward the docks and scowled.

"Oh God."

"Yeah, exactly, oh God. She doesn't want anyone walking on her private rock wall so the kids can't get to the docks and they can't sail. Their big summer race—canceled."

He took a longer sip and said, "She has to be stopped."

"They're just kids," I said.

"First the fancy sand and now this shit," he said, offering me his thermos. I took a sip, not even asking what it was.

"We always watched the race together, as a community," I said.

"The days of civility are over. Now it's just mine, mine, mine," he said. "It's dangerous here with the fence. The kids can't get around it and they can't get out here safely. It's all over." He watched as I drank more and asked, "Are you going to save me any of that or what?"

I handed it back to him. "What is it, anyway?"

"A special blend from the Bahamas. You don't need to know more."

I rolled my eyes at him and turned my attention back to the fence.

"You're right. She has to be stopped," I said.

"Do you want to kill her or should I?" Tuck stared at me with all seriousness and I burped up my drink in fear.

"You look like you could do it," he said.

He took a long swig from the thermos. He stared out across the water and said, "She doesn't even have a soul, so it's not even a big deal."

We both looked across the water at the absence of boats and I said, "A person is capable of doing just about anything when they're desperate."

"That's what I like. A little mystery. What's the worst thing you've ever done?"

"I'm not telling you that," I said.

"It doesn't make you a bad person to do bad things," he said.

"She can't help herself," I said.

"I'm talking about us. I'm talking about you. She's a terrible person every day of her life."

"Why do you keep insisting I'm a bad person?" I asked.

Tuck smiled and said, "I'm trying to tell you that you're not." He turned to me, "I pee all over her sand at night, on purpose. I fight, in my own way. I'm devaluing her property and she doesn't even know it."

I shrugged my shoulders and said, "Seems tame, actually."

He shook his thermos, checking to see if there was anything left. "Don't think I can't be more extreme," he said.

"You can do it because no one will ever tell you to stop," I said.

He smirked at me and said, "I'm a Hoover, not a Kennedy."

"I'm not the type of person who would know the difference," I said.

He turned his bike the other way, toward his house, and said, "I'll let you know what I decide."

"About what?"

"This is my neighborhood, too, Cheryl. I was born here."

He wheeled away without saying another word.

I was worried he was going to do something crazy, but I didn't have the energy to try to stop him. Maybe he was just trying to shift the balance toward the little people.

As I approached my lawn, I noticed that all my plants were wilting and dying. The hydrangeas were parched, the dahlias blooming with dead, browning petals, the black-eyed Susans petal-less. The peonies had been knocked down and were lying on the yellowing grass. I kneeled and cradled the flowers in my arms.

CHAPTER EIGHTEEN

TEDDY

PAULINE AND I WERE going to my least favorite island. It was a dump really, just a gutted-out red barn on some sand and rock in the marshes, only accessible by boat. It was where we had spent our high school summers, stepping through sand with layers and layers of broken glass and other discarded things you didn't talk about. The glass clinked when the small waves crashed in the sand, over and over again like bells.

Pauline shut off the engine of the Boston Whaler and floated it onto the sand next to the other little boats. Six wasted girls were walking in the sand ahead of us. They were already taking off their shoes and I was cringing because I knew their feet were going to get all torn up, but I didn't say anything because I was trying to navigate off the boat with my one good arm. There were lights floating past the broken windows of the barn. Pauline hung back, wanting to kiss me. I was surprised. This is what settling felt like, I thought. I tried and failed to get aroused, so I gave her a little kiss and walked on. All the girls were falling all over themselves to get to the coolers of beer and the guys were pretending to be helpful but just wanted to get into their panties. Don't get me wrong, these girls wanted them grabbing at their panties.

No one looked familiar to me.

Pauline pointed at me, from arm to arm, and said, "Which one?"

I lifted up my good arm and she kept looking at my immovable arm, and I think I caught her grimacing. She pressed something hard and small into my palm and closed it up, then stood back. I opened it and saw a little pill and she smiled widely. Suddenly, I felt like I could love her.

We walked farther down the beach, away from the people, and sat down. I thought about how I could end up with Pauline now. I couldn't believe it. There was something deformed about me that I didn't think I could fix and maybe that was good enough. I slid down onto the sand, getting the seat of my pants wet, but at that point I didn't care anymore. Everything felt wonderful all of a sudden, numb and warm. I looked at Pauline and she was staring at the reeds vacantly, in a holding pattern.

Then Pauline started to touch me and kept apologizing about it.

"I can't help it," she said. I wanted to push her away but no part of me could move. We sat back and stared out at the ocean and I was hoping the tide would come in and take me away finally.

"I don't feel high anymore," she said after a little while. I didn't, either, but I knew it would come back. She started kissing me. I kissed back halfheartedly. No, I didn't think I could love her, actually. Anyone, really. I needed to stop fooling myself about that kind of shit.

She felt around for my penis, but I was flaccid.

I started laughing at the thought. I was flaccid all over. She pulled back, thinking I was laughing at her. It wasn't her at all, I told her. I couldn't even form the words to tell her what was happening, so I just kept smiling and letting out laughter like I couldn't control any part of me. I couldn't. My arm didn't work. My penis didn't work. I could hardly even use my hand to make my penis work. *This is it, Teddy. This is the new you.*

"Why haven't you ever come to see me?" I asked.

Pauline stared at me blankly and said, "What do you mean?"

"You're always up on me, but when I needed someone after the accident, you were MIA," I said.

"It's summer," Pauline said.

"What does that even mean?"

"It means, like, no one wants to be sad in the summer," she said.

"Are you fucking serious?"

"I'm high, shut up. Don't get all heavy on me."

"It would have meant something, that's all."

She started touching me again and said, "I'll visit you now."

"It's too late."

I lay back on the sand and said, "Cover me."

"What?" Pauline asked, confused.

"Erase me off the face of the earth," I said.

"You're so dramatic," she said, laughing

"Do me one solid, will you? Be useful."

"How much?" she asked.

"All of me," I said.

I closed my eyes and waited for her to make me disappear.

"Teddy. This is fucking weird."

"Please."

I said please over and over again.

CHAPTER NINETEEN

CHERYL

JEFFREY HAD COME BACK and moved his things into the guest room in the middle of the night. I walked by the room and saw him bending over his suitcase.

"Are you leaving again?" I asked. "You just got home."

"They need me."

He turned and looked at me, then sat down on the edge of the bed. "Teddy's getting better, it looks like."

"The doctor said it's still a long road," I said.

"But he can do more for himself."

"He can."

"I want to continue our conversation," Jeffrey said. "I can help you get on your feet somewhere. Get you set up until you can handle things on your own."

"Somewhere like where? I live here."

"I mean an apartment," he said. "I can't go over this again." He had finally found someone to excite him again. I suspected there were

pool all the way over here. I gave up after five numbers, unsoothed.

I thought about hotel bars. The upscale ones, with single women, working women on business trips. Families at home that they never saw. Wearing slim-skirted business suits. Or perhaps Jeffrey was meeting locals. Sad packs of women looking for businessmen to take them upstairs, away from baby bottles and babysitters and teething children. They wanted something other than infants nibbling at their chafed skin. He was probably with someone like my mother. I didn't think he'd pick someone like me again. The outlet girl with no obligation to go home to anyone, always convenient and willing. I was always curious about Jeffrey's approach to women. Did he go up to them or did they make the initial approach? Did he play shy or did they? Who else did he promise to pamper?

I slipped my hand into my underwear and imagined Jeffrey talking to a toothy blonde. Asking her name, taking her up to his room. Probably a room with dark wood cabinets with brass handles, the air conditioner turned to 64 degrees, and turn-down service with the television turned on to the channel that played music on a loop and flashed soothing images. He probably asked her if she wanted a drink from the minibar. He would ask her to take off her clothes while he folded his pants neatly over the seat back of a chair. Was she nervous about being with a stranger? Maybe. Maybe not.

When I was finished, I pulled my hand out of my underwear and tucked it tightly in between my thighs. I squeezed as hard as possible, trying to erase my hand. I rolled to my side in a fetal position, feeling everything at once, and began to cry.

I thought I heard someone outside, rustling around in my garden, but I was too tired to get up.

CHAPTER TWENTY

TEDDY

I WOKE UP in the reeds, my pants completely soaked with salt water. Pauline and everyone else were gone and high tide was in full effect.

I got up and started walking around the island. Broken glass was blinking in the sun and sand and there wasn't a single person left but me. What the fuck, Pauline? She didn't care about me. I went inside the red barn and hunted around for anything I could float on. The inside of the barn was gutted out and painted in graffiti. The wood was weather worn.

I sat down on a bench and stared out the broken window of the barn. It was all coming back to me now. My arm was hurting. I needed some painkillers, but my pockets were empty. My fucking phone was gone. This was terrible shit.

Even in low tide it would be difficult to get back to land. I'd have to wait for another party. The only other option was to try swimming with my one good arm. I wasn't even sure what time it was. I stared up at the sun, trying to figure it out, and nearly burned my eyes.

The tide was receding and I tried wading out into the water, but the bottom dropped out beneath me suddenly and I lost my footing, going under for a minute. I flailed my one good arm and it didn't do much. I tried to move my other arm, but it stayed stubbornly limp by my side. I dragged myself back to shore, paddling with one hand through the water, kicking up black mud with my shoes. The water was murky and thick as I crawled back to land. Fuck, what was I going to do?

I looked out at the sailboats on the horizon. They'd never come down here, in the marshes, in the muck. The water was glittering like I'd never seen it before, or maybe I'd just never noticed. Everything looked hyper-colored. The marsh grass was tall and green. I could even hear the chattering of the small fiddler crabs running back and forth across the sand and into their holes. I started throwing empty clam shells into the water, trying to make them skip. One fucking arm. I couldn't remember much from the car accident, just flashes in front of me and me trying to avoid them. It didn't matter anyway. I was never going to be Richard Shepard. I was never going to be my dad. I would have to learn not to be successful. I would have to stop using words like "excel."

I threw a shell and it actually skipped. That small thing made me feel like a human being.

Then the fear that I was going to have to live at home forever with my dad and Cheryl overwhelmed me. Avoiding them both as they avoided each other? She was just getting worse. And when I'd ask her what was wrong, she'd just mutter something about nothing working.

Or worse, what if I had to stay with my father forever, alone? He'd keep telling me to get it together and I'd fucking let myself die.

I lay back and stared at the clouds. I loved doing this as a kid— looking at cloud formations, staring at butterflies—things you didn't tell anyone about. One hand could feel the sand and the other couldn't. It was the strangest thing, like part of me didn't exist anymore. I dropped sand onto my dead arm, thinking back to last night, when I'd asked Pauline to cover me. I wanted to be gone and hidden for once, but it hadn't worked. Neither did pouring sand over my dead arm. I didn't feel a thing, not even a little bit. I thought about cutting it off, but there was nothing around to do it with.

This island hadn't always been a shithole. I used to come here with my parents when I was a kid and people would have family picnics or neighborhood parties here. Back then, the graffiti was just some names surrounded by crooked hearts cut into the wood of the barn wall with pocketknives. I sailed small boats off the muddy waters and pulled their strings to bring them back to land. I'd load the boats with angry crabs and snails and whatever else I could find and spend hours watching the crabs scurry and jump out of the miniature boats and into the water for safety. I watched my mother untuck foil-wrapped dishes of potato salad and corn while my father tried to start the rusting, slanted grill someone had installed on the island. He'd cook hot dogs for us and I'd watch them, my mother's hand on his back, rubbing it while he turned the dogs and think, I could float away and they would never notice.

I walked to the edge of the water, to my old miniature boat launch, and stared out at the water, trying to remember how it was to be around two people who felt that way about each other. There was a piece of plastic peeking out of the reeds and I leaned down to grab it. It was a small, mud-crusted boat with a hole in its side. I washed it in the cloudy water and tried to save it from itself. I tried to make it float, but it teetered to one side and capsized. Cheap plastic shit. When I was a kid, my boats were made of wood and looked like small-size replicas of the real things. I had my dad paint Joanne on all of my boats just so mine could match his. I'd send the fleet out onto the water and watch my mother smile at the sight of her name on all of them. We'd shout "Pirate fleet Joanne come to ransack the islands!" and my mother would hover and yell at the crabs not to jump off, to keep sailing because they had islands to pillage. I'd yell with her. I'd yell to the captain of the fiddler crabs to stay strong, to not lose hope on his journey. It all felt so important then, because my mother made everything feel important. My father would watch us but never join in. It was our game, not his. I missed her. Things felt doomed without her. When she died, I ran to the water and threw all my ships in. I wanted them to go with her, to keep her safe. I pushed them away but the waves kept bringing them back to shore. I finally crushed them under my feet when I knew the tide wouldn't take them away from me. I hid the broken wood in the spaces between the rocks of the breakwater by our house and watched it float in the dark, trapped water.

How could I ever pretend to be brave?

I squeezed my eyes shut because I couldn't think about it anymore. Because I'd have to follow the timeline to right here and now.

I sat down and let the sun burn my skin.

CHAPTER TWENTY-ONE

CHERYL

IN THE MORNING I looked around my room and thought about where I could possibly go. An apartment somewhere? I stared out the window at the water, the big expanse of sky. I wanted to remember all of it.

I opened my drawer and stared at the pile of numbers. I knew a women's mixed doubles tournament was already underway and no husbands ever went to watch, so they were alone at home or shuffling their children in front of cartoons or into sprinklers so they could have some alone time at the computer or in front of the television. I picked out a number and dialed. After the fourth ring I nearly hung up, ready to pick out another, but then I heard a click and swallowed, readying myself.

"Hello?"

When he said it, *it sounded like yellow,* and I got ready. I stopped myself for a moment. Was it Tuck? I had never heard him say hello like that before. It might have been okay.

"How are you?" I asked.

"Who's this?"

I wouldn't tell him and he said, "It's too early for telemarketers, isn't it?" And I could feel him wanting to hang up.

"You sound a little lonely," I said.

He was silent for a while and then he started to whisper, "How would you know?"

I tried to guess whose voice it was, but nothing came to me.

"I just have a feeling, is all."

"You don't know anything about me," he said.

"But I want to," I said, and I meant it. I wanted to make us feel good.

That's all he needed. I could almost hear him unzip through the phone later, when I told him how I was pressing my hand down hard in between my thighs and pretending it was his. I lay motionless as I heard him exhale abruptly, finished.

He asked me if he could see me and I said no and we hung up quickly. I crumpled up the number and flushed it down the toilet to make sure I could never call back.

I looked at my hair in the bathroom mirror and it was greasy and limp. I couldn't remember when I had washed it last, so I turned on the shower and waited for it to warm up. Teddy wasn't home, but that was fine.

The blinds were open in my bathroom and I could see into the Magrees' bedroom, our houses were that close here. I wasn't sure whose room it was, but there was a four-poster bed and paisley sheets and I figured neither of Leslie and Patrick's sons would go for that. The bed looked like any other bed, not a married couple's bed or a surface to have sex on. It was in full view of our bathroom. They could hear the toilets flushing or the shower running or someone struggling to evacuate their bowels if both our windows were open. That was a kind of intimacy I wasn't interested in having with them. So I shut the window, although it was hot and stuffy in the bathroom. The window right behind the toilet was open all the time in the warm weather. What must they have thought of us, lying in bed at night, hearing the bathroom sounds?

Why didn't we hear their sex sounds when we were in the bathroom? Their bedroom looked barren. I couldn't even tell if there was anything on the walls. Leaning in closer, I thought I could make out a Norman Rockwell print. Of course. An old sea captain or something. Not one inch of our homes lacked a beachy feel. I wanted to buy a pink flamingo to put where my flowers had been just to watch the uproar.

Everything had begun to fog and I finally stepped into the shower. My skin wasn't taut anymore. My upper thighs were pocked with cellulite and it made me self-conscious to wear a bathing suit to the club pool, the dips in my skin showing through the fabric. But to wear one of those suits with a skirt was even more alarming. I would go and hope that no one would notice and I'd eye the other women and scrutinize their cellulite and stretch marks. Not out of malice, but to see where I fit in on the roster of female imperfections.

After the shower, I walked around my bedroom naked, even past the uncovered windows. If someone was outside, they could possibly see everything and for a moment that was thrilling. I felt myself strutting, picking up clothing, tucking it into drawers. Who was I showing off for? I imagined I could hear the crunch of gravel.

And then I saw that someone was staring at me from the yard. I ran and pulled a sheet around me.

The room was all windows and I had left the blinds up, on purpose. I walked to a window, sheet pulled tight, and saw that it was Steven, leaning against the fence like he owned it, watching me. He looked hungry, like he'd spend all day in the yard looking at our windows if he had to.

I opened the sheet.

He didn't react—he just stood there staring. I just stood there exposing myself to him, hoping he would react in some visible way. I wanted to say, "You want it."

He smiled and I stared down at him, finally feeling a sense of power again. He needed me as much as I needed him. We stared at each other and I wasn't afraid anymore. I looked down at the shock of my white breasts against the rest of my tanned skin and when I looked back into the yard he was gone.

Later, I put on a dress, something pleasant and cotton that I found in the back of my closet. A-line. Red. Steven was seeking me out and I had to acknowledge that. What I didn't like, though, was that Steven was probably the one killing my garden. Outside, I pulled the dead flowers, my peonies, what was left of everything, and I looked at the ocean. They had wrapped the fence along the seawall. The neighbors on the corner still threw their dog shit into the water. I saw them. The neighbors who barreled their fists into the air, the ones who told Lori that the fishermen were shitting in the water.

I stopped gardening and picked up all the dead plants, conscious of the dirt I was getting on me, and left the yard with them. Older men from the club that I hardly knew were driving golf carts up and down the streets. They looked papery, liver-spotted and veiny. I kept walking and passed the houses on Ocean Beach Avenue with all their bumblebees buzzing and white fences gleaming, past giant black-eyed Susans, azaleas, dahlias, and rose gardens in every shade all bright and blooming. What had I done to deserve a dead garden? Pebbles were finding their way into my sandals and jabbing at the soles of my feet. I pressed on.

Jeffrey had begun to look at my feet and laugh. He called them unfeminine, thick. He was an expert in all things feminine. It was strange at first; I wasn't used to someone knowing more than I did. I'd watched my mother dress, lay out her lingerie, and become beautiful for men, doing the things she knew they liked, and it'd been intoxicating to me. But Jeffrey had been surrounded by it. Boxes of it, old lingerie boxes from the 1950s and '60s stacked in his mother's dress shop. He told me how he'd steal away after school, hide with the boxes and stare at the women and their corseted bodies and bullet bras. I thought about him as a child, hovering over pink-tinted boxes with bouffant-lidded ladies and laughed to myself, imagining him opening the boxes and running his fingers along the lace and stiff boning on the corsets. Even as he told me, his eyes wandered into the dream of it, making him nearly breathless. I wondered if those boxes were the first thing he'd ever masturbated to. Hard pink lingerie boxes with beguiling women modeling 32Cs.

Women were still mysterious to him, even at his age. The smell of them, their movements. He would always be the boy in the dress shop, weaving his fingers through the straps and lace. When we first met, he treated me like one of the women on the lingerie boxes, like an unearthly thing. I became something to marvel at, even under the high fluorescents in a fitting room folding clothes. I became thankful for having the chance to become otherworldly, even for a short time.

I finally reached the Cronins' house and threw the dead flowers on their lawn. Fran was walking out the door in a new visor, one I hadn't seen in the golf shop, and madras shorts. She looked at me strangely. I checked every window, looking for him, but they were all dark and empty.

"Cheryl, what on earth are you doing?" Fran said, walking over to me.

"I brought these for Steven," I said.

She didn't understand any of it and I kept searching the empty windows.

"Did he say he was going to water them and then didn't?" she asked.

"No."

"I just don't know what you expect me to do with these," she said.

I asked her if Steven was home and she went on the defensive, long used to people coming to find Steven, to talk about what Steven had done, to scold her about Steven.

"He's out," she said curtly.

I could see the silk shantung curtains fluttering then, as if he had heard me. I saw his face, I thought.

"Why would you bring my son flowers?" she said.

"He wanted my attention and he got it."

She stared at the dead flowers in disgust, then leaned closer to me and hissed. "What's he done now?"

"Nothing," I said. I only wanted to see how he was doing, I told her, how his face was healing. She tensed for a moment and then fell to pieces. She talked about visits to the plastic surgeon, how Steven used to be so handsome, how awful it all was, and that he was in his prime. Still just a boy.

She looked at her big house and then back at me, mascara smearing. "He's really just a sweet boy," she said, looking down again.

They were all sweet boys.

I walked the long way home, through the hidden parts behind the damaged tennis courts, missing the sound of tennis balls hitting racquets, over to where the golf carts were washed and tuned up. I heard rustling and stopped, then peered around the corner, behind the tennis practice wall. I saw Tuck, leaning up against the wall and groaning quietly, a woman in a short tennis skirt on her knees, all of him in her mouth.

I moved out of view, afraid he might see me. I pressed my face against the painted concrete of the tennis wall and listened to them. Tuck was no better than everyone else, his love for his wife a lie. Who was kneeing the pavement, getting pebbles stuck in her shins? Some other mother from the block? I wanted to know. I flattened myself against the wall, moved my head inches to peer around again, to get a better look. I could see he was near climax, his breaths closer together, murmuring "Oh fuck."

He turned to look in my direction and climaxed when he saw me, and my stomach dropped. I looked down at Tuck's wife as she pulled her face up and smiled at him. I watched as he helped her up, gently stood her against the back of the tennis wall, and dropped to his knees, lifting up her skirt as she stared down at him, still smiling.

I pulled away from the wall and launched myself toward the golf cart garage, red-faced. I stood among the golf carts in the dark and looked back to the practice wall. Finally, Tuck and his wife walked across the parking lot, holding hands. Him kissing her, her arm sliding around his waist. Tuck spanked her playfully as they walked.

I sat in the front seat of a broken-down golf cart and watched them walk toward home. Every part of me rippled with electricity. I felt brittle and unused, but I didn't need to be. I didn't want to feel this alone anymore.

CHAPTER TWENTY-TWO

TEDDY

I COULD HEAR an outboard motor in the distance. It was too good to be true, so I kept my eyes closed. The buzz got closer and I finally opened my eyes. There was a Whaler going past the island. I waved and it came closer. An older guy in a ratty T-shirt and shorts was driving it, beer in hand. He had his sunglasses on a string, like they were going to go somewhere.

"Hey. You okay?" he said.

"No, I'm trapped," I said.

He cut his motor and floated toward me. When he got close enough, I realized it was Tuck from down the block. He grasped at his beer, nearly crushing it in. At this point, I would have taken a ride with anyone. I had been on the island for hours and it would be dark again soon.

"Get in," he said, and I did.

"How'd you get out here?" he asked.

I told him I'd been at a party and he laughed. I was sure he'd been to a few himself. He stared at the island for a while, the gutted barn, trying to remember things.

"I wasn't sure if I'd have to stay there forever or what."

"You would have been living the dream out here," he said. He stared at the island like it was something special. "How are the parties now?"

"The same," I said.

"I spent a lot of good summers getting drunk there," he said. "A lot."

"Yeah, we all did," I said.

"Makes you think, right?"

"I guess so," I said.

"Think about how many layers of glass are on that sand. How many generations of broken beer bottles," he said, staring at the glass-lined beach.

"Sad," I said.

"No, it's fucking awesome. They're like artifacts by now. And one day your generation's beer bottles will be artifacts, too. And on and on."

I was waiting for him to start the motor back up, but I wasn't going to be pushy. He saved my ass, after all.

"Want a beer?" he asked.

He handed me a cold can from his cooler and finally started the engine.

"Something to think about," he said. "Oh, keep that bad boy down. Don't want a reason for the Coast Guard to stop us."

I suspected that that was what you were supposed to say—something to think about. I just wasn't sure how I was supposed to respond. Say "Lots of pussy on that island," or something like that?

"So what, this is like the Grand Canyon of beach party spots? Here long after us and all that?" I said.

"Exactly, man. Now you're talking," he said.

Tuck tilted the boat to the left as he tried to turn it and I clutched the side with my good hand, the hand farthest away from the lip of the boat. I caught him staring and then he said, "Oh yeah," and took another sip of beer.

"I've seen the rise and fall of this place. And watching the generations pass through just warms my heart. It really does. Sometimes I just like to cut out my motor and watch the festivities. Takes me back, you know?"

He was happy living in his past and I couldn't fault him for that.

We rode the water in silence for a while, past the big quarry barges, the trolley bridge, and the bird sanctuary. The outboard made the cranes fly out of the marshes and into the air. I watched them and understood why Cheryl liked walking here.

"How are your parents?" Tuck asked. "You know, Jeffrey and Cheryl."

I knew who they were. I knew he wasn't talking about my mother.

"They're fine."

"Haven't seen them on the golf course," he said.

"My father's been away on business."

"Cheryl must be lonely," he said, taking a sip of beer. Like he was trying to choke back what he just said, like I didn't actually hear it. "What do you think she does all day?" he asked.

"I know what she does. Wanders the house," I said.

"What else?" he asked.

"I don't know. Plays cards at the club. Sometimes she plays golf. Walks a lot. Collects shit."

"Like what?" he asked.

I thought for a minute. "Those little bottles from hotels that my dad brings her," I said.

Tuck stared out at the line of homes like they were specimens.

"She likes to garden," I said.

Tuck nodded. "Yeah, I see her out there sometimes," he said.

Everything on our lawn was dying, so I wasn't sure she was doing a good job. My father would be pissed for sure, when he came home. He was all about curb appeal.

"Interesting lady," he said.

I guess Cheryl did it for some people.

"Things bad with that thing?" He pointed at my arm as if it were some kind of foreign object.

"Well, it's not going anywhere," I said.

He laughed and had another swig of his beer.

"Fucked up," he said while staring out at the waves. I understood that he was trying to be deep, that we needed a moment of silence. I got that about Tuck, he was a deep person.

He was getting closer to the club and I saw the big yachts in their slips, the blue of the clubhouse, the pool. Our houses. The fence was a joke, but all of this had to be protected and we were the ones to do it. Instead of going to the docks, Tuck veered around the rocks and back into the ocean.

"Are you in a rush to get home?" he asked.

"Kind of," I said, but he didn't care.

He weaved the Whaler into the open waters of the sound. I watched the big houses that leaned up against the seawall. The fence created a barrier between it and the lawns. He sputtered the boat to a stop in front of my house and we stared at it, sitting in high tide.

"What are you doing?" I asked.

"What does that look like?" Tuck said.

"That's my house," I said. "I don't know where you're going with this, buddy."

We were both going to start using vaguely insulting names on each other, I could tell.

"This place belongs to us and she thinks she has a right to dictate what happens here. Like none of us matter."

He lost me. Who was "she"?

"What I'm saying is . . . she needs to be stopped."

He stared at the row of houses and shook his head. I was afraid to ask because he was talking like I should know. He looked at me and took another swig of beer. I felt like I had cotton in my mouth and the beer wasn't helping.

"You're totally out of touch with what's going on here, aren't you?"

He was challenging me. "I see the fence, man," I said. I stared out toward the fence and the seawall and tried to determine how far I'd have to go to get to the fence. If I could even propel myself over it. I realized that it was too far and that I couldn't. Before it would have been easy.

Tuck looked exasperated, waiting for me to say something more.

"I'm hearing what you're saying and it sounds like you're pretty pissed off. I understand. I just don't know who you're talking about," I said.

He took another sip of beer.

"Lori Hughes, man. She's bringing us all down. This neighborhood is a sinking ship."

I tried to stay out of neighborhood politics because Cheryl and my dad were always bitching about someone building a too-big garage, or unkempt flower pots, or dog shit, or whatever.

"It starts with the sand and it ends up with putting a choke hold on this whole place. She canceled the sailing race."

I shook my head, confused. He was nearly slurring and I wanted him to stay on topic. "One thing at a time. What'd she do to the sand?"

He cracked open a new beer and said, "Imported it. I saw the trucks myself. Dropping it down, covering up that beautiful Connecticut sand. Who does she think she is?"

I stared at the beach, her house, and said, "I don't know. Someone with too much money." I took another beer. "What do you mean she canceled the race? That's total bullshit. She doesn't have the power."

He was rocking the Whaler back and forth with all his anger and aggression. "Does she own the water that touches her beach, too? Does she own the waves that crash onto her expensive sand?" he yelled.

"I don't think so," I said.

"When does it stop?" He moaned. "How much does she have to own to make herself happy?"

"Someone should do something," I said.

And then he said, "Don't you know it."

I looked at him and knew he was going to be the one to do it. Good old stoner-dad Tuck had finally gotten riled up about something.

We stared at the houses and floated.

CHAPTER TWENTY-THREE
CHERYL

I DROVE AROUND IN CIRCLES for hours, up and down backcountry roads, through small immaculate towns with quaint Connecticut-town names. Past old-town creameries serving cups and cones to small children and apple orchards with rows of trees brimming with new fruit. I thought about early autumn orchard fairs and hayrides and apple cider, warm and steaming. I thought about hiding in far-flung rows of apple trees with boyfriends as a teenager, rolling around on rotting fruit, not caring at all. It was hard not to see all my life choices on a loop.

Finally I ended up in front of my mother's house. I drove up and down the street at first, and then parked in front. Her driveway was empty and there was a For Sale sign in the front yard. The windows were no longer covered in tinfoil. I could see inside if I wanted to. I looked through the windows and saw furniture and rugs and rooms filled with things I remembered. I tried the door and it was locked. The broken window had been fixed. I wasn't going to try to smash it again. My hand had finally healed. I was starting to feel frantic being so close to the remnants of my life but unable to touch them. I walked around the small garage and tugged at the heavy rolling door.

It was musty inside and full of broken pieces of brooms and vacuum cleaners and other household things. Things my mother should have thrown away. I stood in the garage, inhaled the spores of dust and mold. The concrete floor was covered in layers of faded oil spots, some probably mine, and I thought about my mother's old Datsun that I used to drive around, looking for some excitement in this small town. I remembered there was a spare key to the house here somewhere, I'd hidden one for the times I'd try to sneak back in after my mother had kicked me out, always looking for a way back in.

I looked through the cobweb-covered paint cans on the shelves, checking under each one. I knew none of them had been moved since I left, so there was a chance. There was always a chance. I found the key hidden under a box of nails and screws. It had been untouched for so long, the outline of the key was imprinted on the wooden shelf. My hand shook as I walked over to the metal-sided door and pushed the key into the lock. She wouldn't be in there. What was I afraid of? The door opened and the dusty air moved as I moved through it and clouded around me. I stood in the kitchen and didn't know what to do except stare at the ceramic orange jars that had held cookies and treats for us as kids. I opened them and found them empty and had to sit down. Everything was just as I remembered it, but vacant. A shell of a memory.

If she had died, I wanted to know where it had happened. Was it in here or was she doing something mundane like shopping at the supermarket? There had been no mention of her in the papers; I'd checked. Maybe she wasn't dead. Maybe she just got up and walked out of her life one day. I left the kitchen and walked through the living room and stopped. The furniture was the same, musty nubby chairs and a faded leather couch. Something new and strange inhabited the house, though. Dozens of Virgin Mary statues crowded the mantel. Some

CHAPTER TWENTY-FOUR

TEDDY

IT WAS NICE HAVING a break from my father, I had to admit, but all I wanted to know now was when he was coming back. He hadn't answered his cell in days. I was starting to think something had happened to him and I didn't know why I wasn't doing more about it.

I ducked behind the parking lot and then the bushes that ran along the snack bar and stood there for a while. Kids with swimmies looped around their arms were walking with their babysitters and the babysitters were mediocre-looking. I was itching to see Jill. I thought a dip would feel nice because I hadn't showered in days and a crust of salt had formed on me.

I didn't feel like talking to anyone at the pool, any of the young girls who looked at me above their stupid books that had young girls in sunglasses on the covers. They wore small white bikinis and were toned and blond and thought they looked really hot. All the men around them, old enough to be their fathers, thought so, too. They golfed with the fathers of these girls and jerked off about them in the clubhouse bathroom. I knew, because I could hear them, alone in the stalls. These girls crossed and uncrossed their legs, layered Hawaiian Tropic oil on themselves to glisten brighter and attract attention to their boobs and that thin ridge in between their boobs that I liked a lot. These girls didn't look at me anymore. I was invisible to them now, with my limb hanging limp at my side, muscles eating themselves minute by minute. My other arm was already dwarfing my dead arm in size and it made me look lopsided. I hated them then—those girls pretending to read and really just hoping to be another image in the family friend's spank bank.

I took a towel from the waiter and felt thirsty. I couldn't carry both a towel and a drink. I couldn't anymore. I had to carry one or the other. Or try to lasso it around my neck. Or tuck the towel under my arm and squeeze it tight while I tried to maneuver the spout of the water tank to spill water into the plastic cup and nowhere else. It all seemed impossible. I thought, *This is how it's always going to be.* I would only ever do one thing at a time.

I tried to lay the towel down on the chaise with the wind blowing; I almost had to ask for help. I pulled off my shirt and felt people watching me, as if they wanted to see how I would do it. I kicked off my shoes and leaned back on the chaise. The sun was nice and for once I felt safe. I closed my eyes and listened to the children scream and play.

I saw a shadow cross over me and I opened an eye. It was Jill, folding a towel down over the chaise next to me. She was already stripped down to her bathing suit. I felt my penis move. I was getting aroused and became very self-conscious. A girl once told me that the best way to get rid of a hard-on, or to make one last longer, was to think about ham sandwiches. Build the layers—the pieces of bread, slices of ham, cheese, tomatoes, lettuce, the mustard on top—and get really involved in the ingredients. Visualize putting the thing together. You could go on making ham sandwiches for minutes, then look down and realize you were all right. I looked down. There was hardly a stir. Jill turned around and looked at me and I saw the white part of her breasts, the part that hadn't tanned this summer. I wanted to cry.

"I didn't see you there," she said.

She flopped down next to me and tried to assemble the pool toys at her feet. Foam noodles and plastic throwing stars, shit I used to play with as a kid, too.

I tried to shield the sun from my eyes so that I could get a better look at her. She looked tired and annoyed, not like the other times. She had a trashy book beside her. The cover had a man grasping at a half-naked woman with plump lips and huge breasts.

"Is it any good?" I asked.

She looked down at the noodle, then her book.

"Lots of heavy petting," she said.

"I figured," I said.

She stared at the book, and I knew she felt the need to defend it more.

"Sometimes you just need to shut your brain off."

Then she stared at the pool and her children flapping around with their swimmies on.

I wished that she could have come up with something more insight-ful, but this was it. Tired housewife who may or may not have hated her kids. There was no forced sandwich-making necessary. I closed my eyes again. I could hear people talking, but they weren't talking to me, so I fell asleep.

I felt my face burning hot and someone shaking me awake. I opened my eyes and saw Jill there.

"How long have I been asleep?" I asked.

"About fifteen minutes," she said.

Why had she shaken me awake? She smiled when I asked her.

"I was bored by the book," she said, and then, "So few weekends left to sit out here."

I groaned because the summer was ending. It was over. It would get cold soon.

The bored women would go back into their houses, shut themselves in, and wait for next summer when they could take off as many clothes as possible and try to make a go of it. Take chances again. She was quiet for a moment. I pushed myself up trying to wiggle the back of the chaise up; she leaned over and tried to help me.

"You don't have to," I said, feeling like a child.

"Why don't you come watch me anymore?" I thought I heard her say.

I turned to her and she smiled. "I kept hoping you'd come back," she said.

I felt a buzzing in my ears and I wasn't sure how to answer.

We both stared at the pool.

"Do you love your kids?" I asked.

"Of course. What kind of question is that?" she asked.

"Would you ever leave them?"

She looked at me and laughed. She said, "For you?" Jill put her sunglasses on and waved to her children, who waved back with a lot of excitement. She was waiting for me to say something else. I could see her little smile from where I was sitting. I didn't want to sit there anymore. I started getting up.

"Don't go," she said quickly.

I slid back into my seat. People were looking at us, or was I just being paranoid?

"Why are you doing this?" I said.

"I'm not doing anything," she said.

"I wasn't watching you," I said.

"You were."

She put her book down.

"You're reading too much of that shit," I said.

She was quiet for a moment and then slid the book under her seat.

I closed my eyes, hoping she'd disappear. I didn't want her to start telling me about loneliness or missing husbands or shitty kids. None of that. I didn't want her to talk anymore.

"What do you want me to do?" she asked.

I didn't know how to answer.

Leave me alone, stay, touch me again.

Things like that popped into my head, but I didn't say them.

"Nothing," I said finally.

We lay there, side by side, staring at the pool full of children.

I opened my eyes and Jill smiled at me and said, "Let's go to the rocks tonight. I'll get a babysitter."

I said okay and she left and I had to go wait for her. Hours still.

When I got home, Cheryl was in the garage, shuffling around. I asked her what she was doing, but she didn't answer me, didn't even register that I was there. I called out to her again and she finally looked up. I didn't feel like telling her about my ordeal. I didn't want her to think I was a fuckup again.

"What are you trying to do?" I asked.

"There's a hurricane coming."

"Maybe we should call Dad," I said.

The phone in the kitchen was off the hook.

I ran back outside.

"I need help with these boxes if you have a second."

It was so bright outside, but in the garage she had found the shadows and was hovering in them.

"Maybe you shouldn't open those," I said.

"It's all just junk."

I stared at her, trying to get rid of it all. She told me, "We have to board up the windows."

Cheryl came into the light and she was smiling. She put her hands on her hips and looked around the garage.

"Spring cleaning a season late," she said.

I asked her if she had talked to my dad and she said she had and he was going to try to make it back before the storm. I was glad there was something that was actually making her worried and that she wasn't acting crazy because she was going crazy. Everyone on the shoreline was afraid of storms.

She held up some *Playboys* and *Hustlers*, my father's collection, and said, "Maybe we could board up the windows with these?" She was smiling when she said it, like everything was a big joke.

"We could show them what it's all about, right?" she said.

She flipped through a *Hustler* magazine. "Why are they always wearing pearls?" She looked at me as if she expected an answer. She held up the magazine and showed me a woman with her legs spread wide, no underwear but with a bra on and a long string of pearls around her neck. I had no idea, but the magazine had to be from the early '80s. They still had hair in dark Vs.

"You should probably put that down," I said.

Cheryl continued to thumb through the magazine.

"I remember them being worse," she said.

She put the one she was holding down and picked up another one, a *Playboy* from a long time ago.

"We always had these around the house when I was a kid," she said.

She hardly mentioned her past and I wanted her to say more, but she never did. When she first came home with my dad, I had no idea where he had found her, and at the wedding no one came for her at all. My dad had told me that her family was poor, broken apart, that she had *risen above it all.*

They said they wanted to keep it small. People were still mad at my dad for leaving my mother and Cheryl wanted to move quickly. My father hated being alone, so he didn't ask any questions. Then, after my mother died, the neighbors got even more pissed. I was pissed, too, but

I knew Cheryl was just another victim of my dad's whims.

Now, here she was, rifling through his things. She picked up video-cassettes and held them out.

"What do you think are on these?" she asked. She stared at the black cases. "I can't make out what the scrawls say. Your father always had horrible handwriting."

I didn't want to see anymore. I didn't think she should be looking, either.

"Come on, Cheryl. Let's talk about this." I held my hand out for her. She dropped everything back in the box and followed me out.

"Are you hungry?" I asked.

"A little," she said.

I put my arm around her and walked her inside. Her hair looked disheveled and I wasn't sure when the last time she'd showered had been. I put her to bed in her clothes and she didn't fight me. I went to call my dad.

I had a few more hours before I could meet Jill. Exhausted, I dialed my father's number. It rang and rang and he didn't pick up.

I hung up the phone and tried again. And again.

I turned on the TV, flipping through channels and looking for the storm. It was in the outlying islands around South Carolina. A man in a rain slicker was being battered by rain and wind. I stared at the sky and couldn't imagine that it was headed our way. Why wasn't anyone else panicking? The weatherman said it would probably miss us, veer right and head out to sea. There was only a slight chance it would make its way to New England. That was what they were saying.

The only thing I could do was go upstairs, push through the bottles of shampoo in the drawer, and get to my pills.

I went to lie down.

There was a banging outside the house that startled me awake. I looked out the window and there was Cheryl, hammering nails into the house and trying to put up pieces of wood to cover the windows. It was hard to watch. I felt foggy, like my legs weren't going to move much further. I needed to get ready. I moved one leg in front of the other and went toward the shower. I didn't have the energy to stop her and I didn't want to be late.

CHAPTER TWENTY-FIVE

CHERYL

"WHAT THE HELL is going on over here?" Jeffrey asked.

My skin began to itch and I had that cold feeling that I felt sometimes when Jeffrey would get loud.

"I've been calling for hours," he said. "I have nine missed calls from Teddy."

"Why didn't you call him back, then?"

"I did. I just said I've been calling." He looked at the mess at my feet. "What are you doing in the garage?" he asked. "Why are you going through my boxes?"

I told him I was preparing for the storm, someone had to. No one else seemed to think there was anything to worry about. He told me to come inside and I followed him.

"How was your trip?" I asked flatly.

"Not long enough," he said.

"There's a hurricane coming up the coast. I'm surprised you made it," I said. "I've been thinking of options, possibilities."

"Well, it's not here yet."

He made himself a drink in the kitchen. A triple, I think. I was hoping he had reconsidered. I was hoping for some tenderness. Or maybe I should have just changed the locks.

"Do you think it'll be bad?" I asked.

"I don't know," he said.

We were silent then.

"I have nowhere to go, Jeffrey."

"I'm sorry," he said. But he meant it out of pity.

There were different ways to be humiliated, I thought then.

He asked how Teddy was and I told him I had just seen him, but nothing of the circumstances.

"Did you tell Teddy yet?" Jeffrey asked.

I shook my head. I wanted to walk into the ocean and swim away like those people who could cross channels by sheer willpower. People with that kind of inner strength amazed me. I lacked faith, though.

"I'm afraid," I said.

"We've been through these things before. It'll be fine." He walked over and refilled his drink.

I had been through hurricanes before. Great big ones, ones with hail the size of golf balls and all the things that weathermen on TV warn you about. Hurricanes with names that sounded benign—Andrew, Gloria, Belle, and Bob. When we were children, my mother would let us stand out on the porch to watch the lightning storms go by. Sometimes we'd run to the lake, my sisters yelling as we raced through the storm light. I had the longest legs and was the fastest. We'd try to find a hiding place under a tree or next to some brush so that the lightning couldn't get to us. We would lie and wait for the bright lights to shatter down through the air. Sometimes, we could see bolts jumping from cloud to cloud and would reach our arms up just enough to frighten ourselves. We could hear our mother calling out for us in the distance, calling us back.

Telling us to be careful. My sisters would shove me out of their hiding spots and leave me to fend for myself. I'd lie down in the sand, at the edge of the water, and wait to be hit. They'd call out to me, yell for me to move, but I'd lie there, just waiting with my eyes shut tight.

I could hear their voices still. "Cheryl, you're going to get hit. Cheryl, you're going to get hit!"

I didn't care. Didn't they know that I wanted to get hit?

"I don't know why people are ignoring this storm. Especially after last year," I said.

I walked to the window and looked for dark clouds. The sky was blue, unnaturally so. I could feel myself pretending with him, but the possibility of being let out right then, like a squatter, made things too difficult to face at that moment.

"I don't see any clouds, though," I said.

"Is this how you're going to try harder?" he asked.

"How are *you* going to try harder?" I countered.

"I didn't say I was."

He was out the door before I could say anything, taking his drink with him. I picked up the phone and dialed Steven's number, hoping he would answer. The line rang and then I heard a crackle, a near moan. The feeling of doing something illicit when Jeffrey was close was thrilling. I could get back at him in a small way.

"Hello?"

It was him. I glanced at the windows to see Jeffrey standing and looking at the ocean.

"I'll be surprised," I said.

He asked when and, nervous, I checked the windows again.

"Before the storm."

"Okay," he said.

I saw Jeffrey urinating on what was left of my flowers. I couldn't believe it. He had been doing it all along. He zipped up and walked away, down toward the rocks. I hung back and tried to process the cruelty. He knew how much I loved my flowers. Then I heard shouting outside and hung up the phone. It sounded like Jeffrey, so I went back to the windows but couldn't see anything. I followed the sounds outside.

Jeffrey was standing on the end of the seawall, drink in hand, his hair whipped into a frenzy by the wind, yelling at someone. I watched them, close enough to hear what he was saying. He was pointing at one of the new No Trespassing signs and yelling at Mrs. Humphrey, who spent most of her time in Florida and was rarely seen outside of her yard even when she was in Little Neck Cove. She had the house nearest the rocks, and she had made it her business to make sure no undesirables walked along her wall.

She was screaming at Jeffrey to get off the walkway. She said, "Don't you see the signs?"

He said, "Fuck you, woman. I live here."

I didn't think I heard him correctly. He was talking to a neighbor, not some person on the street. She said she was going to call the police because he was trespassing on association property. He screamed that he belonged here as much as anyone else. And then he started trying to rip the No Trespassing sign out of the ground. Mrs. Humphrey disappeared into her house, but Jeffrey did not stop yelling.

"You fucking cow, come back here!" I saw the security guard who had been there the night Teddy had his accident approach Jeffrey. Jeffrey lunged at him, screaming, "YOU!"

Then two police officers came through the Humphreys' yard and Jeffrey started yelling at them, too. They tried to reason with him at first, asking him to move away from the water's edge. He refused to get off the seawall.

He said, "I pay my taxes. This is my walkway, too."

Mrs. Humphrey said, "I've never seen this man in my life. He's trespassing. He's a vagrant!"

"You cow!" he screamed.

I nearly laughed and nervously checked Lori's windows to see if she was at home, if she could hear the commotion, but they were dark. Jeffrey looked wild, almost young with anger. The police moved toward him and he swung his arm at them, missing by a wide space.

"Calm down, sir."

"Don't tell me what to do."

"Let me see your ID," one of the officers said.

He told them he wanted to see theirs. They asked him if he'd been drinking and Mrs. Humphrey yelled that he had thrown a glass at her. She used the words "assault" and "scared."

"I'll kill you if you come near me," Jeffrey screamed. "I was here before you bastards were even born!"

I inhaled sharply, knowing that was all they needed to hear.

They tackled him then, driving his face into the grass of Mrs. Humphrey's yard. I thought about her two little corgis and hoped they had used that spot to urinate—the spot where Jeffrey's nose was being screwed into the ground by the hand of a policeman. I could hear his muffled yelling and almost convinced myself that I could feel the reverberations coming up through my feet. I did not move. Not even when they picked him up and put handcuffs on him. He tried to struggle away from the police, but they were much stronger.

He screamed that the neighborhood was turning into a police state. "I have rights, too," he said. "Why are you handcuffing me? I'm just taking a walk."

"Public intoxication and trespassing," they told him.

I could have helped him, but I didn't. I could have strolled over and said, "I'm his wife and we live nearly next door." But I just stood in Lori's yard behind her row of evergreen bushes and watched as they treated him like a criminal. I took comfort in the fact that none of us were safe—the fence was closing in on us all. Jeffrey stopped fighting and hung his head down as they led him through Mrs. Humphrey's yard to their police car. For all his screaming, though, he never mentioned that he had a wife. He never asked them to come find me. It was as if I didn't exist to him; we had become each other's afterthoughts.

I ran from Lori's yard back to our house and to the front windows. They put Jeffrey into the backseat and I watched as he sat there staring at the houses as if he'd never seen them before. He saw me staring at him and we locked eyes. He looked ragged, like an old man who had wandered away from his house in the night and was found confused. He started to say something in the backseat of the car and it slowed. I pulled away from the windows, hid in the shadows, and watched as he nudged his face toward the house and where I was standing and said something over and over again. The car came to a stop in front of our house and Jeffrey shook with fury. I panicked. He knew I deliberately hadn't helped him, that I had allowed his humiliation to go this far.

The car rolled forward again and I watched it go quickly down the one-way road. I came back outside then.

He was gone and I was glad.

"What happened?" Lori said, as I turned around. She was red-faced and confused, power-walking toward me with weights in her hands.

"They just arrested someone," I said.

"See, see!" she said, pointing at the fence. "God, it looked just like Jeffrey."

"Well, he's gone now," I said.

"All this happening here. Christ," Lori said. "I'm going to alert the security guard to keep an eye out for him, make sure he can't get back in here."

"Good idea," I said, and smiled. "Ready for the storm?"

"You know, the kids get so nervous. We're probably going to go to a hotel. No sense in riding it out. Who knows after the last few. You guys?"

"I'm staying until the end," I said.

CHAPTER TWENTY-SIX

TEDDY

AS I WAITED FOR JILL on the rocks, I thought about what I had just seen. They were really coming down hard on outsiders, and now some-one had been pulled off the wall and hauled off in handcuffs. He was in hysterics and it was kind of funny to watch. The lady on the corner had cracked down on people walking near her house; all she needed now was a moat. Instead, she had to settle for big-ass signs threatening police action if you came near her house without permission. I couldn't remember it ever being like this. When we were kids, we rode bikes around, left them in neighbors' yards, and swam in the ocean, running down beaches that didn't belong to us. No one ever tried to stop us. The neighborhood was ours. Now it was nobody's. Each yard was bar-ricaded in with fencing. We just needed some Dobermans patrolling at night and we'd be all set. They could really make this a gated community and have guards at every street entrance checking IDs and bank account balances, like they did with the really rich. What was so wonderful to protect, anyway? The boats, the docks, the clay courts, their precious eighteen holes?

It was high tide and the water was hitting the rocks and spraying me. Usually I'd get pissed and move, but I had the best view of my house from where I was sitting. I searched the windows, trying to catch a glimpse of Cheryl. Any movement at all. There wasn't any. I pushed myself back and put my head on the rocks and waited. Jill had picked the right time, the sun would set and it would be nice. With everyone finishing the golf tournament and celebrating with booze and trophies afterwards, I didn't think anyone would see us. Even if Cheryl did, I didn't care. Who would believe anything she said? I saw a family on bicycles stop at the gate, afraid to go farther, past the fence. I didn't recognize them, so I didn't feel bad. The fence was doing its job. You're not welcome here, but have a nice day.

The fireflies were gone and summer was winding down. The club was rushing it with the golf tournament, the members sipping vodka out of their plastic cups with bendy straws. They would have to piss out there, hidden in the fescue, because of their prostate problems. It seemed pretty strange to be paying a thirty-five-thousand-dollar entrance fee only to possibly get a tick on your penis as you tried to hide the stream from the riders in the carts beside yours. It didn't seem that simple pleasures like that would be afforded to me anymore. I wouldn't get to swing anything, not anymore, right? None of this would ever be mine.

When I disappeared and went somewhere else, I could play up the disability and have people take care of me. Heartstrings and all that stuff, right? It was a possibility. Before, the best I could get was a job selling shit like my dad. Hawking medical equipment, pacemakers and those things that beeped in hospitals—the heart monitors, that's where the big bucks were. I would have started off in pharma, selling to doctors, one of the only salesmen in a sea of big-titted blondes with fake tans who pretended to know the difference between Advair and whatever the fuck else they sold. Endless tests to make sure I knew everything about drug interactions, chemical makeups, all that. Now I wasn't going to do any of that. I was going to be handled differently, like I couldn't do things. And I had to decide if I was going to take it or not.

I didn't have to do anything anymore or pretend that I had some kind of calling.

Cheryl put kind of a kink into my plan of riding this out forever. My father would be pissed when he got home. Divorce probably. Or a slow burn of quiet, which they were already well into. I was blood and no one was throwing me out. She would go away, like the other ex-wives from the neighborhood, forced into a tidy condo in town, ousted out of the club. They didn't take kindly to single-lady competition here. Married couples in some state of misery or single men with liver spots. That was it. I didn't think Cheryl deserved a fate like that. I really didn't. She was different from the others, and really not that bad. She took care of me even after I spent years treating her like she didn't belong in our breaking-down home.

I saw Jill coming. She was wearing a short white dress again. I hoped it was see-through, especially with the sea spray still going strong. Even though I knew I would only get so far with her, no matter how bored she was in her marriage.

She waved at me and walked down the seawall quickly, careful not to fall when she reached the rocks. She was wearing some kind of cork shoes and held both arms out to steady herself. I got up to help her and she took my arm and smiled.

"Thanks," she said. I nodded, suddenly very nervous. Her dress looked like a sack sort of, but it tightened around her breasts. She made everything look good. She leaned in to kiss my cheek and I could smell her. Sweet flowers, like the kind around here hanging over the white fences.

She pulled away and I asked her what the kiss was for.

"A hello and thank you," she said.

She stared down at the rocks and tried to figure out how she was going to sit down. The seagulls dropped oysters and clams down on the rocks to break them into pieces and there were shards everywhere. I leaned down and scraped them away, trying to make her a seat. She sat down, folding her hands behind her ass and pressing down as she sat, so she could have some fabric beneath her.

"You missed quite a show," I said.

"What happened?"

"This crazy guy was trying to vandalize the No Trespassing signs. The police came and hauled his ass off," I told her.

"There's too many signs now."

"How many would be enough?" I asked.

"I don't know, honestly."

I thought it might be time to round up the guys to fuck shit up again, but most of them had moved away to start their lives already. Only Steven was left. I wasn't sure if he was up for it anymore. Besides, he'd probably burn her house down for fun. No one really understood the true extent of Steven's appetite for destruction unless they saw it firsthand.

Jill stared out at the ocean, at the setting sun, and smiled. "This is nice."

"It's pretty good," I said.

"I never come over here anymore because it's all blocked off."

"It wasn't always like this," I said.

She murmured that she knew.

"I bet the sunsets are nice over here," she said.

"Girls like it," I said.

She turned and smirked at me.

"Everyone does," I continued.

"Everyone does," she repeated.

We stared out at the water and I wasn't sure what to say to her anymore or what she wanted from me. Right now she just wanted to sit next to me and stare into space.

"What do you think will happen?" she finally said.

I didn't know what she was referring to and I hoped it wasn't some kind of big, philosophical conversation starter.

I said, "I don't think the storm will hit us."

She turned back to look at the sky.

"Maybe it will," she said.

I went into how the weatherman said it wouldn't, that it was already in South Carolina, but she wasn't listening.

"Do you want to go somewhere else?" I asked her. She shook her head.

She asked me where I lived and I pointed to my dark house. Only the lights in the living room on the first floor were on.

She wrapped her arms around her legs and I asked her if the mosquitoes were getting to her. She shook her head. Was she giving signals for me to put my arm around her? "Where's your husband?" I asked.

"Out there."

She pointed behind her to the course. They would have to come in around dark, probably go upstairs to the Captain's Lounge to have a few scotches, pat one another on the back and talk about their handicaps.

I nodded my head and watched the sun drift down. She looked down at my hands, my limp one in my lap and the other one I was using to steady myself on the rocks.

"Does it hurt?" she asked.

I looked down. "I can't feel anything," I said.

"Nothing at all?" she said. She leaned in and kissed me.

"I can feel that," I said. I kissed her back.

She pulled away and said, "Good, what about this?"

She reached out to touch my hand, my arm. I couldn't feel it. She pressed her thumbs into my skin and I saw the white imprints when she released it and then watched as they quickly disappeared. She pinched me and I didn't move.

"Stop," I said.

She tried to pull my hand toward her, to touch her, to see if I'd flinch or move away, but I didn't. She put my dead hand on her leg and I was sorry that I couldn't feel anything. She had little blond hairs on her tanned legs; I wanted to feel those but couldn't. She put her hand on my pants, where my penis was, and it barely registered. She pulled it away quickly.

We looked at each other and she smiled at me like she was sorry for me and I wanted to pull my hand off her leg. I could have used my good hand to pull the dead one off, but that would seem to show even bigger weakness, so I didn't move at all and she kept smiling at me. Finally, she gave me my hand back and jumped up.

"How did you know I watched you?" I said.

She turned to me and her hair fell onto her lips and she stared at me, real deep, and I turned away.

"I saw your car. Then you," she said. She looked down at her smooth legs.

"Why didn't you let me in?" I said it as a joke, but she considered it.

"If I knew that you'd stop showing up, I would have."

And then what, I wanted to say. And then what? The breeze picked up her short white dress and I could see a flash of flesh-colored under-wear. Full fabric—I was curious why she didn't wear thongs like other girls. Maybe it was an age thing.

I reached out and slid my fingers under her underwear and let my skin touch hers and felt the goose bumps rise. She let me touch her for what felt like minutes. She was smooth and soft, and when I pressed down I could feel the muscles she got from hours of playing tennis. She felt spectacular. Jill slid away from me and sat back down and put her hand over mine. We stared out at the sun until it was nearly gone. This was the best I was going to get.

She turned and smiled at me, then said, "Do you think they're finished playing yet?"

I said, "Maybe you should just go over there now."

She looked at me a little hurt, but we were now both aware that nothing was going to happen and that this wasn't fun anymore or cute. I wasn't sure what she was expecting, maybe for me to start showing up again, hiding in the jungle gym, hoping to get a glance of her. She got up and brushed off her dress, then put her arms out again as she moved over the crab carcasses and broken pieces of clam shell.

"I'm sorry about what happened to you," she said. She touched my arm and it felt like something she would say to her kid, not someone she had just kissed.

CHAPTER TWENTY-SEVEN
CHERYL

I WAS ALONE in the house and everyone was gone, the TV was set to the Weather Channel, and the meteorologist was bleating about high winds and storm swells in Cape Hatteras.

Then he said, "Unlikely to hit the Northeast," and I was crestfallen.

The phone started to ring and I stared at it with terror. I knew it was Jeffrey and that he would ask why I hadn't saved him. He would demand that I pick him up, pay for letting him be humiliated like that. I pulled the phone out of the wall to make it stop.

What was I going to do? I couldn't run. I was afraid of what would happen when Jeffrey came home. I locked every door in the house and went upstairs. With no storm coming my options were limited.

I ran to the bathroom and looked through the drawer with my shampoos, slipped my hand past the Hilton Hotel's generic products, and found Teddy's pill bottle. It was empty. I looked around, couldn't believe it. I even went through his room, checking under dirty clothes, rifling through drawers. Searching pants to no avail. They were gone.

No one was preparing because there were still no indicators of the coming storm in the sky. I pulled the small statue of Mary out of my purse and held it, rubbing the robes, checking for chips. There were none and I let go of my breath. I had hoped for some slender cracks, chipping paint, to feel age. I wanted the statue to be something more than a factory-made trinket.

CHAPTER TWENTY-EIGHT

TEDDY

AFTER JILL LEFT ME, I went back to the house and didn't want to go inside. I tried my dad's car and it was locked, so I went to Cheryl's and found a spare ignition key above the back wheel in one of those secret key holders. I hadn't really driven since the accident, but it was either leave or sleep in the car. I needed a drink. I hadn't had a drink in days. I wasn't even sure how I was surviving. I drove around for a while along the road that led from Little Neck Cove to Graves Point. It curved along the rocks and the water came up right to the fence during high tide. The sun was gone and the sky was a dark blue. The houses on the islands stood out black and empty against the sky.

I finally drove to Milligan's and took a place at the bar. It was slow. I looked around, trying to figure out why no one was around. I didn't want to ask. Guinnesses started to appear before me and I didn't ask questions. I was there for hours, long enough to drink six beers at a steady clip, anyway. The baseball game was over. The Yankees had won, and whoever was in the bar left pissed off. I paid my bill and wandered outside. I stood at the edge of the marshes, the smell of salt water thick in the air. In the woods across from the gravel parking lot I used to catch fireflies as a kid. We'd ride bikes there, a line of us pushing one another with taunts to get there faster. We had small traps our mothers made us, glass jars with tinfoil on the top with holes pressed in with forks. We held onto them as we maneuvered the handlebars. We were experts by then and could do this with ease. We'd throw our bikes down in the grass and run into the woods, afraid to miss even one. We swung our arms wildly and put each captured light into our jars. By the end of dusk our jars were all glowing phosphorescent yellow and we slowly rode home, careful not to drop them, watching the lights bounce around as the fireflies frantically tried to escape.

That was what I missed.

Then I felt an intense pain in my face and I dropped to the ground. I didn't have time to catch myself, so my cheek hit the gravel.

What had hit me?

Who had hit me?

Above me stood a sea of pastel colors. They took turns kicking me. Every time I opened my eyes I could see the moths fluttering around the glass globe hanging over the door to Milligan's. I didn't even fight it. No one tried to stop them, not even me. I took it. I heard things like "my children," "cocksucker," and "faggot." I had to laugh at that one and that just made the kicks come harder. I lay there wondering who was kicking the shit out of me and calculated that there were probably about five legs kicking at me with varying degrees of intensity. Some of these guys were actually pretty weak. I bet I could kick harder if I tried, if I was upright. My laughter elicited a move to use fists to quiet my giggles. If I hadn't been so drunk, I probably would have been crying from pain. Crying for my mother. Crying for my dead dog, Maxwell. Wishing I had learned to be brave. And then . . . he leaned down. I knew this because a shadow stretched over the light and he whispered in my ear, "You fucked my wife." I wanted to tell Jill's husband that I wished I had, that I still could.

I should have to deserve a beating like this. I should have fucked his wife for this. Instead of just jerked off to the thought of it. And then a warm, wet glob of spit hit my cheek and slid down past my mouth. I lifted my head slightly and saw that he was wearing navy corduroy pants with small red lobsters embroidered on them.

I would have thought that someone in Milligan's would have called an ambulance or asked me if I needed help. I contemplated crawling into the nearby marsh, trying my luck with the sea, but I just lay there like an impotent asshole. The one fight I'd been in in my whole life and I was blindsided by five assholes and never even got in one hit. I couldn't even embellish the story and say I think I got one of them. I didn't get any of them. They all got me. Their pent-up upper-middle-class aggression was taken out on me. I'd be whispered about at parties and lobster boils, at male-bonding experiences. I was going to have to clean myself up and get in my car and go home and bang on the doors to be let in, and when my dad got back I'd have to tell him that I got my ass kicked and that I didn't even get one hit on them. Not one.

That would be added to the story they told—the story about how these men recaptured their masculinity. How they felt alive again, dangerous and strong, erasing all the years their wives had been emasculating them. Except they weren't going to say it like that. They were going to say that I stuck my dick in one of their wives and they were fighting for their family. Protecting their family against someone like me. And look who was going to come out looking like the asshole. One-armed me.

I got up and hobbled toward Cheryl's car. Everything hurt except my bad arm and I laughed as I cradled it. I had done my good deed for the summer, giving Jill's husband and his friends reason to slap one another's backs again, walk a little taller, and fuck their wives a little harder. I had done them their great big favor. I had reminded them that I was the weak one, not them.

CHAPTER TWENTY-NINE

CHERYL

I COULD FEEL MY JAW each time the air pressure changed now, that certain ache that made me rub the bone line. If I had Teddy's pills, I wouldn't have to feel it anymore. I lay in bed with my arms stretched wide, the way you sleep when no one is going to come and disturb you. I thought about Steven and our connection and how lucky I felt to be wanted again. Like I had gotten a second chance at something and no one could take it away. He seemed so needy, like me at his age. If I had found someone who cared so much about me then, I wouldn't be here now. Would that have been better? How could I even ask myself that question?

I heard the front door open and braced myself. I heard movement downstairs, as if someone was searching for something. I did not move, my body tense as the footsteps started up the stairs.

I thought about calling out, pretending I was surprised by the intrusion. I closed my eyes quickly as the footsteps moved down the hall toward our room. I heard them stop in front of the other rooms. Doors

opening. Then he was standing in front of the open door to the bedroom and did not move for a while.

I heard footsteps creaking toward me and I squeezed my eyes shut harder, like when I was a child and I didn't want my mother to know that I was listening.

The footsteps stopped next to the bed and I waited.

I could feel the weight of him in the air beside me and kept my eyes closed, not knowing what he was going to do.

"Can I lie down next to you?" Steven asked.

I opened my eyes wider than usual, trying to muster surprise, and he liked it, I could tell. I moved over in the bed and he slid under the sheets fully clothed. He leaned in close to me and I could smell the detergent on his clothes.

We faced each other, heads on the pillow, and then he pushed my shoulder, wanting me to turn over, and so I did. He pulled me toward him, nuzzling his face in my back. I just lay there, listening to him breath and feeling his warmth, our legs entwined together. He clutched onto me as if being this close was a necessity for life. I looked at his skin next to mine, hoping for some miraculous change, but all I saw were my sun-worn hands against the kid-hair on his soft arms and it was devastating.

"Will you help me?" I asked.

He murmured yes against my back.

Teddy woke me up in the middle of the night, banging on the front door, covered in blood. Steven had left sometime before, but his imprint was still in the bed and I knew then that I had not imagined him being there.

I nearly had to carry Teddy to the bathroom and while he was showering off the blood, that's when I saw the TV reports that the storm was going to hit us after all. It was a Category 3. It could move to a 4,

maybe even a 5 if the perfect conditions arose. Then they started calling the conditions "perfect."

Later, when the storm came, no one was prepared for it because of all the false reports from previous years. It was worse than the forecasters had imagined. The water was rising rapidly and it was clear that the seawall wasn't going to keep it back. There would be evacuation centers with cots and food set up at the Warren G. Blake Middle School. The checkout lines at the grocery store stretched back into the aisles and men from the meat department had to direct traffic inside the store. They ran out of bottled water in less than an hour. People were talking about where they should go, unsure where to take their supplies. They were bracing for the worst, with little more than party-size bags of corn chips and Doritos. Children piled in the fruit snacks as if they might be their last packages on earth. Inland hotels and motels filled up quickly and there was talk of price gouging at the gas pumps in nearby towns. Police on TV said they would be investigating the reports.

I watched as Lori stood in her driveway, her arms loaded with pillows, and yelled at her children to take their dogs and get into the SUV. They just stared at her, unmoved. I wondered where her husband was. His car was already gone.

Later, I looked outside again and saw Tuck pedaling toward the water. I moved from window to window watching him. All the families had fled by then, but he propped his bike against the white fence and walked out along the seawall as if no catastrophe was looming. He walked with his head tucked down, the wind flattening his hair against his skull. I watched him from the front windows. He stared out at the ocean, watching his boat being tossed around in the waves. Then he stretched his arms wide and began to flap them like wings, like he was trying to fly away. I laughed in spite of myself. Then he turned around and stared at my house, at the window I was standing in, laughing. I watched as he ran back to his bicycle and rode off, and I wasn't sure how he was able to stay upright in the wind. He stopped in front of Lori's house. She had been careful to have all the windows boarded up and he jumped off his bike and hurried toward them. I watched him try to pull the boards away with his bare hands, but they did not budge. He disappeared into her garage and I waited for a few minutes, wanting to see what he would do next.

He came back with two golf clubs, a driver and an iron, and lodged the iron between the nearest plywood-covered window and the house. He ripped the covering off and took some of Lori's expensive shingles down with it, then used the driver to smash the glass. As he went from window to window I thought about intervening, but Tuck was doing this for all of us.

He crawled through a window, then came back out through the glass doors, leaving them wide open. He got on his bike, saluted to the ocean, and rode away.

After checking on Teddy, who was still passed out on his bed, I went through the abandoned neighborhood. Some windows were covered, but most weren't. My attempts at readying the house had failed. I power-walked past the Cronin house, trying to keep my hair out of my eyes. The wind and rain were brutal. The lights were off and in the fading light I couldn't see if Steven was there. I went into their yard, to the side door, and jiggled the door handle. It was locked. I looked around flower pots, rocks, mats, trying to think where Fran would leave the key for herself and others.

Her geraniums were slightly askew. I peeked underneath and a small rusty key was sitting in a thin layer of dirt. When I put it in the lock I had to jiggle it a bit but it worked.

The door swung open and the mud room smelled like spoiled potpourri. I didn't hear any movement in the house, so I pressed on. The living room had plants in strategic places, but they looked too shiny and well maintained to be real. I didn't see any dry bits or dead parts. I touched the leaves: they were fake. The wind had picked up outside and it made the glass in the windowpanes rattle. I started moving through the house quickly.

I went up the stairs and stopped in the hallway. All the doors were closed. It seemed so cold to me, to have each room cut off from one another. The bathroom was the first door on the left. I walked in. It looked like it had just been redone with new wood paneling. I pulled open the drawers. They were empty. The house didn't seem lived in to me. Where was the mess? The bits left behind?

I spied Fran's visor on the towel rack. The one thing out of place. I took it, stared at myself in the mirror, and put it on. It was tight, but it brightened up my face. The pink brim hid the fine lines and wrinkles running along my forehead. I adjusted the strap as snugly as I could and left the bathroom, careful to shut the door behind me.

With the brim of the visor shading my eyes, I had to be careful how I walked.

The next door was the master bedroom. I looked through Fran's closet but nothing jumped out at me. She only wore muted tones, and mostly strange linens. There were cropped pants and shorts on hangers. I closed the door behind me when I walked out. Steven's room was at the end of the hall. It still had stickers left over from his adolescence—STAY OUT and GUARD DOG—stuck to the fake painted wood.

I hesitated. Would he be in there? Perhaps he hadn't fled the storm; maybe he was going to come back to me. I stopped and considered what I was doing there, then I put my hand on the knob and turned. He wasn't inside. It was empty and looked much like Teddy's room. Messy and almost unfinished. I heard a crash outside and moved quickly, rifling through Steven's things.

I sat down on his bed. Things happened on this bed. I could feel it. I pulled back the dark blue comforter. His sheets were stained with dried semen. I bolted up and pushed the comforter back in its place. Didn't Fran ever do the laundry?

It was time to go. I looked up and saw Steven standing there, blocking my way.

"Why are you wearing my mother's hat?" he asked.

I touched it but didn't answer.

"Where did you go?" I asked.

"My parents wanted me to evacuate."

I was so excited to be this close to him, I could hardly stand it. He came near me with his hand outstretched and there was a crash outside.

"Do you want to do it here?" Steven asked.

I closed my eyes and let him walk around me. I thought about being next to him last night and how that warmth had felt like a cocoon. He put his hand on me and I flinched.

"No," I said.

He moved his hands under my shirt and tucked them under my bra, leaned in and put his face on my neck. I could feel his breath, hot and wet against my skin as he breathed openmouthed. I whispered what I wanted him to do to me and he nodded like he understood.

There was another crash outside and I jumped, nervous and suddenly self-conscious in his teenage room. He wouldn't let me go, though.

"I don't want to," he said.

I told him what I wanted him to do again and finally I pushed him off me.

I ran past him, down the stairs and out of the house. I stopped to put the key back under the geraniums then took off again. He didn't stop me. The wet sand covering the concrete parking lot made strange squishing noises as I power-walked through it and up Club Parkway to survey the damage. As I neared the clay courts, I mar-

him and stepped out onto the soaked lawn, he hit me in the back of the head as hard as he could. I heard the same crunch I had heard on the nature trail and was suddenly blind with pain. I touched my head and it felt wet and sticky. I turned to look at his moving mouth, but all I could hear was a soft buzzing sound.

The next wave pushed its way into the house and took us both. Our ribs cracked and snapped under the weight of the water as it pulled us out onto the front lawn and out to sea. All around us, the waves ripped open homes and garages, pulling out soccer balls, trash cans and recyclables, wood pieces from projects unfinished, alongside lamps and winter coats, dining-room chairs, expensive kitchen mixers, and IKEA-bought paintings.

At first Steven fought back, and I saw him thrown around, as if weightless. He gasped for air as his arms crashed through the water. I wanted to tell him to stop resisting, to just submit. Instead, I kept my mouth closed as long as I could and let the water carry me. He swam against the current, back toward home, as I floated out to sea, past large black garbage cans and hollow plastic bowling pins, children's toys and all the detritus of our lives. I watched it all, pain in my head, blood clouding my eyes.

The water rose through the tennis courts, ruining all of the repairs. It made the golf carts that had been tied up with chains float like buoys. In the marshes, the only things that were unharmed were the tall posts with the bird nests atop them. The egrets watched as the water rose up around them and they rose up in kind, gliding through the sky. The water completely submerged the graffitied rocks and rolled over the trolley bridge like it was nothing.

Our yards eroded into the sound as the concrete wall that had kept the water at bay for generations broke into pieces and floated away. Whole gardens disappeared, and soon after our houses joined them. The homes with the best views came apart as if they were made from glued-together balsa wood, crashing down on themselves. The fence went next. Long, white, and plastic, it jerked and spilled right into the murk.

I felt a tangle of seaweed around my ankles as my arms slipped under and then I let the water envelop the rest of me, down into small tornadoes of glittering broken glass. As the waves crashed and receded, I knew I could finally disappear.

ACKNOWLEDGMENTS

The idea for *The Invaders* has taken many incarnations over the years and the themes in the novel have been burrowing away in me for so long I'm not sure what I'll do now that I've let them out.

First and foremost, I want to thank my wonderful and remarkably generous teachers and fellow students in the Columbia MFA program, including Sam Lipsyte, Christine Schutt, and Gary Shteyngart, who helped me grow as a writer.

Second, Heidi Julavits, Ed Park, Vendela Vida, Andi Winnette, Casey Jarman, Andrew Leland, Ross Simonini, and my entire *Believer* family whose direction and dedication helped me become a better writer through learning how to be an editor. I learned from the best.

I would like to thank Kirby Kim for always being on my team and Ron Hogan for his wise edits.

A number of brilliant and kind people read drafts of this novel and gave me invaluable advice and support during the process. They are: Dominika Waclawiak, Jennifer Gann, Roxane Gay, Randa Jarrar, Anisse Gross, Iman Saleh, Diane Cook, Megan Abbott, Sara Gran, Libby Burton, Mark Waclawiak, Janne Darata, Natasha Stephan and my mom. Thanks to Jen Cox, Alyssa Barrett, John McElwee, and Lee Ellis for their general moral support.

My mother and father inspire me every day and I thank them for all of their help, especially my badass mother, who is the kind of woman I aspire to be.

Finally, immense gratitude to Jon DeRosa who is always my first and last reader and is someone I am lucky to know. I am constantly in awe of your talent and curiosity. Thanks for everything.